Celeste

by
Ann Evans

Celeste
by Ann Evans
Published by Astraea Press
www.astraeapress.com

CELESTE
Copyright © 2014 ANN EVANS
ISBN 13: 978-1500982492
ISBN: 1500982490
Cover Art Designed by AM Design Studios

*For Jake and Megan who are old enough to read this now
and
Brennan, Sam and Nathaniel who will enjoy it in years
to come.
Keep on reading!*

Chapter One
Déjà Vu

MESSAGE > Create
Me again. Thnk goin mad. Mum wants me 2 c doc. (sad smiley) > Send

Megan Miller clutched her mobile phone like it was a lifeline to sanity. Texting Katie, wishing she were back with her mates, where life was normal. Where she wasn't hearing things and seeing things.

Where she wasn't being haunted.

She lay on the sofa staring blindly at the TV, insane thoughts running through her head. Trying to make sense of what had happened to her over this last week.

Was it only a week? It seemed a lifetime.

Her mobile tinkled out its familiar little tune and the line *1 new message* appeared on the screen. She pressed View.

Mayb u shud. Poss u r stressed coz of movin hse & sch.
Miss u Katie xxxx (big smiley)

Megan closed her eyes. That wasn't what she wanted to hear. She wanted someone to understand and believe her. Now even Katie, who had been her best friend, thought she was crazy — and she didn't even know the half of it.

Looking back to the day she and her parents arrived here in the city should have warned her. She'd been positive she had been here before, despite her mum saying she hadn't. Of course then, those feelings of *déjà vu* hadn't seemed particularly important — odd yes, but not important. Everybody experienced *déjà vu* at some time or other. It didn't necessarily mean they had lived before, did it?

She'd never believed in reincarnation — only now she wasn't sure. Everything was confusing and frightening.

****

A week earlier, M6 southbound.

Megan's mobile buzzed and the words *1 new message* appeared across the little screen.

"You're very popular today, Megan," her mum remarked, glancing back over her shoulder. Dad was at the wheel, humming along to some rock song on the car's CD player.

Megan took one earplug out of her MP3 player where she'd been listening to some real music. "I can't help it if my friends are missing me already."

"Who's this one from?" asked her mum.

Megan pressed View. "It's from Katie. She says she's looked on the Internet at my new school and it looks a dump." She groaned at her mum's horrified expression. "Chill! I'm only joking. She says it looks like my old school..." Her voice trailed away as the horrible homesick feeling came back into her throat.

Yesterday had been awful, saying goodbye to all her

mates, making promises to text and email each other every single day, but it wasn't going to be the same now. How could it be?

Her mum smiled sympathetically. "It'll be alright, Megan. You'll soon make new friends. If it's any consolation, it's the same for your dad and me. He's starting his new job and I won't know a soul. And it's a lot harder to make new friends when you're our age, believe me."

"Why?" asked Megan. "Don't friendships mean as much if you're only fourteen?"

"That's not what I meant and you know it."

Sighing, Megan tucked her corn-coloured hair behind her ear as she plugged her music back in, missing her friends more than she ever thought possible.

She closed her eyes as her music ran through her head — it was a song about lost love. That was something to be grateful for, she supposed. Leaving a boyfriend behind would have been a killer, bad enough leaving all her mates.

As the car journeyed on she must have slept, because she awoke with a jolt as her mum tapped her knee. "What?" she asked, puzzled.

"I said, we're nearly there." Mrs. Miller looked anxious. "I do hope you're going to like the house we're renting for the time being. It's just until we get a feel of the city, then we can buy a place that we all like."

"It's not home, so it's going to feel weird whatever it's like," Megan murmured feeling utterly miserable, thinking how sad and empty their house had felt as they'd finally closed the front door for the last time.

She bit her lip, staring blindly through the car window, trying hard not to cry. Her dad had done all the house hunting, travelling up and down the motorway for weeks on end, sorting everything out for them to re-locate from the North East to the Midlands.

She pressed Create Message, her fingers tapping out her

thoughts to Katie.

Feelin sooo homesck. Missin u. (crying smiley) > Send

Ahead lay the sprawling city, their new home. A concrete jungle. She'd heard the phrase, now she understood what it meant. It was a mass of concrete, brick and glass, a mix of old and new — office blocks, flats, and old church spires.

Megan stared at the three church spires on the horizon and the strangest feeling swept over her. She sat bolt upright. "We've been here before!"

"Well I certainly have," remarked her dad. "I've been up and down this motorway like nobody's business these last few weeks."

Mrs. Miller glanced over her shoulder again. "You've never been here, Megan. You must be thinking of somewhere else."

"Yes I have! I'd recognise those spires anywhere. You've seen them before too, Mum — you must have."

"Yes, on my trips here with your dad, but you definitely haven't been here before, I guarantee it."

"I must have!" Megan argued. "I know this view. I recognise it from, well… ages ago."

Her mum shook her head. "Sorry Megan, but you're wrong."

"Well, how freaky!" Megan frowned, flopping back. It all appeared so familiar. She knew those spires. But even weirder was, for a minute the ache of homesickness, which had stuck in her throat since leaving home, had vanished. For a minute she wasn't homesick any more.

Just the opposite — it had felt like she was coming home.

Chapter Two
Magic and Sorcery

East coast of Ireland 840 A.D.

They stood in a circle around the stump of oak. Thirteen men in pale grey hooded robes. Hands joined to form a complete circle around the wizened tree trunk. The tree had been struck and destroyed by lightning decades before. Woodcutters had cut through the charred trunk and discarded the withered branches, leaving just the base. It served well as an altar.

The rings showed the oak to have been centuries old before it was stuck by the streak of fire from the sky. Now the wood was stained black by the blood of sacrifices over the years — oxen, sheep, chickens.

On the altar, close to the latest sacrificial offering, lay a pendant. A pendant cast in iron and inset with gemstones. It was no bigger than a man's thumb and formed the shape of a cross. In the centre was a garnet, blood red and a powerful protective force. Inset along the four lengths were honey brown amber crystals and jasper with layers of red, brown, and white — again for protection. At the four tips of the cross were four small hematite stones with their opaque red sheen that merged against the grey of the iron in which they were set. Truly a fearsomely powerful mix.

The pendant lay on the charred oak altar, soaked in blood, encircled by thirteen robed men gifted in the art of magic and sorcery. Above, the new moon cast its silvery glow over the woodlands and a shaft of light glinted directly onto the pendant, making it glow.

This was the moment — the only moment in their lifetime — when the earth and moon and stars were aligned, drawing on the power of nature. It had to be tonight.

One by one, each man raised his right arm and pointed their right index finger directly at the pendant. Each man's eyes squinted in concentration as they focused mind, body, and spirit on the pendant. No one doubting that this sorcery — should it work — would bring anything but good. No one then imagining the jealousy and greed it would give birth to.

The chant started slowly and softly. The spell woven by the elders of the Aes Dana tribe rippling like water until it rose as thunder...

Eternal life grant onto him who wears the Cross of Aes Dana.

Eternal life grant onto him who wears the Cross of Aes Dana.

Eternal life grant onto him who wears the Cross of Aes Dana...

Chapter Three
A Friendly Face

Megan's new school was similar to the one she'd left behind — a busy, sprawling Comprehensive, no bigger and no smaller than her old one. It was just all the faces that were different.

It was odd wearing a royal blue and grey uniform instead of bottle green. It felt weird and wrong and the ache of homesickness was back with a vengeance.

Mrs. Miller drove her to school on her first morning despite Megan's protests that she could quite easily walk there once she'd discovered where it was — but her mum had insisted. When her mum left her at the school gates, Megan had felt like a five-year-old again and had to fight back the tears.

"I'll take you along to your new classroom," the Head, Mrs. Golightly said, smiling briefly before marching down a main corridor which led to another corridor and then another which all looked identical. The *clip-clipping* of her low heels made a mockery of her name but it was obvious that the kids either respected or feared her as they made an effort to either greet or avoid her.

She knew her stuff though, Megan realised. Mrs. Golightly seemed to know every single one of her pupils by name — and misdemeanour — as she rattled out comments along the way.

"Wearing make up again, Vivian? What have I told you? Richard, shirt tucked in, if you don't mind. I know it looks cooler out, but rules are rules. Alison, homework in on time this term please."

It went on and on, pupils streaming by in a hazy blur, faces merging with one another. Megan felt sick with nerves and the horrible sensation of loneliness and isolation was suffocating her.

"This is your classroom, Megan," Mrs. Golightly informed her, leading the way into a room filled with strangers. She spoke to the teacher. "Your new girl, Mrs. Lovejoy, Megan Miller."

The teacher looked younger than Megan's mum and she beamed a big welcoming smile. Now she did suit her name, she looked full of love and the joys of life.

"Megan! Do come in and join us. If it's any consolation, I'm feeling like a new girl too. I didn't have this class last term, so we'll all be getting to know each other."

It wasn't any consolation, but Megan answered out of politeness. "Yes, miss."

"Now then," pondered Mrs. Lovejoy. "Where shall we put you?"

"She can sit by me, miss!" someone chimed out.

Megan scanned the sea of strangers. Boys and girls of her age, all staring at her, sizing her up, judging her, deciding whether she was friend or foe. One or two were whispering; others were smiling. And then one face. One face shone out from all the others, and Megan's knees buckled with shock.

Oh there you are Ruth! Megan almost cried out in delight, a huge smile breaking out across her face. *There you are! It's been so long since I saw you.*

The next second, she halted herself. Stopped herself from falling over her own feet to reach the girl with short corn-coloured hair and dark eyes. What on earth was she thinking about? Who on earth was she thinking about? She didn't know the girl! She didn't know anybody here.

But just for one split second, she had such a feeling of recognition it left her trembling.

"Thank you, Freya." Mrs. Lovejoy put her hand lightly on Megan's arm, indicating for her to go and sit by the girl who had spoken — Freya.

Freya? Where on earth had she got the name Ruth from?

Megan wove her way around the pupils and desks in a daze, unable to stop staring at Freya, her heart pounding madly yet she had no idea why.

****

Freya Mason sat at her desk, feeling quite sorry for the new girl. She had looked absolutely petrified when Mrs. Golightly had shown her into the classroom. She was glad she'd spoken up when she did. For a second the new girl — Megan, had looked so relieved and happy that Freya felt like she'd done her good turn for the day. Oddly, it had made her feel good too. She couldn't remember when anybody had smiled at her so warmly. It had only been for a second however. The new girl's smile had vanished as quickly as it had appeared, as if she were suddenly self-conscious. Now as she threaded her way between the desks, she looked quite stricken.

Watching her, Freya noted that the new girl was slightly taller and thinner than her — but then wasn't everybody? Her hair was long, drawn back in a pony tail but quite similar in colour to her own. Her eyes were brown too, which was quite unusual as most of the blonde girls in class were blue or grey-

9

eyed. Her uniform looked stiff and brand new and she looked as uncomfortable in it as she probably felt.

Freya tapped the chair next to hers and smiled at the new girl. "Hi! I'm Freya — Freya Mason."

****

Reaching the vacant desk Megan couldn't take her eyes off Freya Mason. Vaguely she was aware of the other kids staring at her, two girls sitting in front turned to smile, and a good-looking boy with an elaborate pattern shaved into his hair winked, but Megan's eyes were fixed on Freya.

Where did she know her from? And why on earth did she think her name was Ruth? Yet she reminded her of someone so strongly, especially her smile — the way dimples appeared in her cheeks. It was all so familiar to Megan that her throat ached.

"Don't I know you?" she finally blurted out, feeling such an idiot now. What on earth must the girl think — what must everyone think? The way she'd grinned like a Cheshire cat when she'd first spotted her. The way she couldn't stop staring — even now. She groaned, wishing the floor would open up and swallow her.

Freya gave a little shrug. "I don't think so. Are you on any social media sites?"

"No, I don't do those," Megan answered dragging her gaze away from Freya in the pretence of opening up her school bag.

"Have you just moved to this part of the city?" Freya whispered as the teacher called the register.

"New to the city totally," Megan answered quietly. "I'm from South Shields on the North East coast. We've moved down here with my dad's work." She felt light headed. The strangest sensations were washing over her. It was almost like Freya had been someone she'd been looking for... someone she had been missing.

There you are.

That's what she'd almost blurted out. *There you are!*

****

At break-time Megan was glad that Freya stuck by her, making it her job to show her around the school. She walked with a kind of skip to her step and even that seemed familiar to Megan. She tried not to dwell on it as Freya introduced her to the other kids in class, explaining where everything was, who everyone was, and generally bringing her up to scratch on who was nice, who was spiteful, who was a gossip, and who was likely to steal your boyfriend — if you had one. One boy from their class seemed to think he was a contender.

"This is Jamie Monkman," Freya introduced the tall, gangly boy who seemed to leap out of nowhere on the playground and stood smiling broadly. "But he's weird so ignore him."

Freya said it with a twinkle in her eye and Megan flashed a brief smile in Jamie's direction, recognising him as the boy with the pattern shaved into his hair, although she couldn't see it now with his jacket hood up. Somehow she guessed it wasn't just his haircut that made him weird in Freya's eyes. But no doubt she would explain if she wanted to. "Hi! I like your hair. I noticed it in class."

"Thank you, Megan Miller. And thank you too, Freya for the compliment. Who wants to be ordinary and boring anyway?"

Megan was amazed that he'd remembered her name, and she was about to say so when Freya linked her arm, steering her towards a group of girls from their class.

"Come on, Megan, come and meet Yvette and Sonya. I usually hang out with them, they're really nice."

"Not as nice as me," Jamie remarked, loping along

behind them. He was tall and slim with deep dark eyes that were hard to resist gazing into.

"Not as wacky as you, you mean!"

"Weird, wacky, the compliments just roll off your tongue."

Freya rolled her eyes at Megan — making Megan catch her breath. She knew that expression so well, too. This was crazy! She tried to blank it from her mind as Freya introduced her to her mates, but as they chatted, Megan couldn't stop glancing at Freya, desperately trying to think whom she looked like.

She still hadn't figured it out by the end of the day. But the thing that surprised her most as she headed home was the fact that she'd hardly given her old school a second thought all day.

Their new rented house overlooked an open common. From her bedroom window she could see a stream and a pathway that led way off into the wooded distance — and on the horizon stood the ancient church spires.

Again she felt the odd sensation of *déjà vu*. She had definitely seen them before despite what her mum said. And this *déjà vu* thing was starting to become really annoying.

"So how was your day, love?" her dad asked as they sat down to dinner later. "School okay?"

Megan shrugged. "Yeah. My teacher is nice and I've got to know some of the other kids — but it's really weird, the girl I sit next to, Freya Mason, well, it's like I know her from somewhere..."

She stopped herself from blurting out that it was more than just knowing her. It was as if she'd been missing her.

"Well the way you kids all dress, you're like peas in a pod anyhow," her dad remarked.

"School uniform, dad!" she groaned. "Anyway I'm talking about her expressions and mannerisms. It's doing my head in."

"It'll come to you," said her mum. "Oh! Have you noticed, I've wired up your computer. It's all working perfectly: internet, emails, printer — who's a clever girl then?" She flashed a self-satisfied smile at Megan's dad who raised his eyebrows in relief that it was one less job for him to do.

After dinner, Megan checked her emails, pleased to see loads from her mates. She tapped out replies, wondering what Katie would say about the feelings of *déjà vu* she'd had.

It wasn't long before a reply came back. 'Send a pic. I'll see if I know her. Missing you! Katie xx'

'I'll try. Missing you too.' Megan emailed back, feeling quite guilty because amazingly, she wasn't missing anyone.

Wandering over to her window, she noticed a boy throwing a ball for his dog on the common. It looked very much like Jamie Monkman and as she watched, her curiosity grew as to why Freya thought he was weird. He'd been quite friendly to her in a clowning kind of way. And he was certainly nice to look at. That afternoon, she'd asked Freya, but Freya had just groaned and said 'don't ask!'

Checking her computer for any more emails, she finally turned it off and went downstairs to watch TV for a while. After that it was off to bed — an early night, she decided, school in the morning. And tomorrow, maybe she'd figure out who exactly Freya Mason reminded her of.

Chapter Four
Between Two Worlds

Black fog swirled around him. Long-dead eyes peered out through the eternal gloom. Echoes of death and decay coiled in suffocating density about his dark spirit as he wandered the ancient long-gone corridors and cobbled city streets.

Hell should have claimed him centuries ago, but his curse and oath as the noose tightened around his neck as he hung from the gallows, had robbed the devil of his soul. But he was left in the blackest of purgatories.

Through the mist, figures came and went — demons usually — wanting to know if he was ready to be taken down to his destiny. He cursed them aside. Hell would have to wait. He glimpsed other figures at times. They swept by his dank, black world as if on the wind. These were living, human figures, as he was once. Few had the sensitivity to notice him and those who did paled and grew sickly with fear.

That was his one pleasure now, to creep out from behind the swirling black mist that surrounded him, to haunt those mortals who lived and breathed.

He had found a way that he could, with the greatest of effort, summon up the mist, gather it in one arched doorway-shaped mass — and walk through it into the living world, returning the same way.

For now, he paced the empty dark corridors that had once been Godgifu's priory, oblivious to the majestic cathedral that had been erected overhead.

He walked, head bowed, his cowl shrouding his face, although his eyes bore through the black mist, forever watching, waiting...

Although true hope had died a long time ago, still a thread remained.

And a doorway...

****

School the next day was fine. In fact Megan enjoyed the rest of the week. Each day she got to know more people, although Freya was never too far away, nor Jamie come to that. However Freya seemed to have taken her under her wing — keeping an eye on her. It was a nice feeling, Megan realised — a comforting feeling.

On Friday afternoon, as school ended, Freya asked if she fancied meeting up in town the next day. "How about it? Shop till we drop and do some touristy stuff around the old medieval part of the city as well."

"The haunted bit," Jamie interrupted, appearing like he always did, suddenly, out of the blue, making you jump.

Freya flashed her brown eyes at him, a frown crinkling over the bridge of her nose. Megan stared fascinated. She could almost see Freya clenching her little fists and stamping her feet — which was really stupid.

Yet, somewhere at the back of her mind, there was a memory. Desperately, she tried to recapture it, but it remained elusive. Frustrated she concentrated on Jamie, irritated by the sensation of *déjà vu* but quite pleased that Jamie seemed so interested in her.

Freya however, glared up at him. Standing with hands on hips, the top of her head barely came up to his shoulder. "Jamie, an elephant would be proud to have ears like yours! This is a private conversation. Must you always stick your nose in?"

"She loves me really," he said, grinning, and looking directly at Megan. "Freya and I go back a long, long way."

Freya groaned and rolled her eyes heavenwards. "Don't start! Megan doesn't want to hear your weird ideas."

"But she should, in fact…"

"Jamie, shut up, will you? Megan and I are planning our day out in town. That's her and me, not you — before you ask! This is a girly day out."

Jamie cast Megan a woeful look and stupidly her heart flipped. "She never used to be like this y'know. Anyway, if you're going sightseeing, be sure to look around St. Mary's Hall, and the Priory ruins and the cathedrals obviously. Now if I was coming with you, I could give you the low-down on all the old buildings and the historic characters who used to live there, and those still hanging around — in a haunting kind of way you know. It would be far more interesting."

Megan actually thought it was a good idea, but the look on her friend's face said otherwise. She smiled at him. "Another time. We'll probably be looking round the shops mainly."

"Shopping? Not my scene," Jamie announced, swinging his school bag over his shoulder and pulling up his hood. "Have a good weekend. I will see you on Monday." He strode off, his long legs covering the ground until he'd caught up with some boys who were more welcoming than Freya had been.

Their relationship intrigued her and as they strolled towards the school gates, she asked, "So, what's between you and Jamie?"

"Oh! He's just weird. He infuriates me at times because he talks such a load of old rubbish."

"About what?"

Freya sighed then looked wide-eyed at her. "Well, if you must know — reincarnation! The crazy boy thinks he's lived before."

"You're joking! When? Where?"

"Oh, he's been a Viking, a monk, a Tudor toy maker — you name it. He even says he remembers me from a past life — can you believe that!"

It sounded fascinating, but obviously Freya thought differently, because a moment later she had changed the subject to chat about a fantastic pair of shoes she'd seen in town last week and how she hoped they'd still be there tomorrow. Megan listened to her chattering on about them, but deep down her thoughts were on the curious and gorgeous Jamie Monkman.

****

On Saturday morning they met at Broadgate in the city centre just before eleven. Megan couldn't help noticing the bronze statue of a naked woman on horseback. "That's Lady Godiva, isn't it?"

"Yes, it is. Well done! So you know something of our history," said Freya, giving Megan a nudge, suggesting she look behind just as a clock chimed the hour. "Bet you've never seen anything like this before though — it's dead classy!"

On a building opposite were a large clock face, an arched window, and a small railed balcony with arched doors either end.

"Keep watching," Freya chuckled.

The doors slid open and a white wooden horse with a naked rider hobbled around a track, moving slowly and jerkily towards the open doors at the other end. The next moment the arched window above slid open and a wooden head with bulbous eyes peeped out, ogling the naked lady.

Megan shrieked with laughter. "Oh my goodness!"

"Bet you don't have anything that impressive in your old town!"

"No, thank goodness! What's it all about?"

"Well, Lady Godiva was supposed to have ridden naked through the streets of Coventry to force her husband, Leofric to lower taxes…" Freya stopped and pulled a face. "Megan, just be glad Jamie isn't here or he'd be boring you with the alternative version, of how naked could have meant without all her finery, rather than without her clothes. And how her name wasn't Godiva at all. It was Godgifu — gift of God."

Godgifu!

The name drifted through Megan's head like an echo from the past. Without thinking she exclaimed, "Godgifu wouldn't have ridden naked. She was holy and good…" She stopped in mid flow. Why on earth had she said that? Yet the name Godgifu sounded so familiar. And with the name came the impression of holiness and goodness — and suddenly a face. The face of a woman etched in sadness and weariness.

Startled by this sudden and crystal-clear image in her head and the depth of emotion that came with it, Megan stood rigid.

Freya was still chattering on. "There are different opinions on the legend, but there has to be some truth in it because Godiva built a huge monastery so she must have been religious. Oh well, who cares? Shall I show you those shoes?"

"Yes, great," Megan murmured, still puzzled about her knowledge of Godgifu. And whose face had just popped into her head from nowhere?

As they explored the shops, Megan just couldn't shake the face from her mind.

It was a woman in her early thirties, with sad, sad eyes.

Her mouth was moving, saying words she couldn't hear, holding something out to her. But what it was, she couldn't see.

The shoes Freya had liked were gone, so they wandered around the stores, trying on other shoes and different outfits. Later they bought jacket potatoes smothered in grated cheese and sat on a bench eating them while pigeons strutted around their feet.

"Are you missing your old friends much?" Freya asked as they ate.

"It's funny, I thought I'd miss them like crazy, but it's not been too bad," admitted Megan, stopping herself from ranting on and telling Freya that their friendship had filled a huge gap. Then afraid that Freya might read her thoughts and think her a bit funny, she showed her some photos on her mobile. "These are my best mates. We've been texting and emailing non-stop. They're all pretty mad!"

Freya studied the photos then handed the mobile back with a smile. That indulgent 'I don't mind smile' that Megan knew so well. "They look good fun."

Megan wanted to scream. Why did she keep getting these crazy *déjà vu* feelings? It was driving her insane.

Somehow she hid these thoughts and kept up a normal conversation. When they'd finished eating Freya was keen to show her the touristy sights. She led the way to the medieval area of the city.

"Y'know what," Freya remarked, as they strolled down a cobbled street towards the cathedrals, "We could actually do with Jamie now as our official tour guide."

"He knows his history then?"

"Oh yes, especially the bits he thinks he was part of," said Freya with a groan. "Some of these ancient bits go back almost a thousand years."

Freya's mobile started to ring then and so Megan dawdled on while she answered it, thinking it would have been nice if Jamie was here, and not just to talk about history. Although a thousand years — it was such a long time. Yet things still stood, like these old buildings, these old narrow streets. The cobbles were red and shiny, washed bright from a recent shower of rain. Everything glistened and shone. It was easy to imagine how the old city would have looked. A market place here, people selling wool and leather; townsfolk and travellers and black-robed monks; donkeys and chickens, horses pulling carts, their wheels clattering noisily, market stalls brimming with vegetables; all the pungent smells and chaos of a bustling market town.

She wandered slowly on, waiting for Freya to catch up. Ahead stood the orange sandstone shell of the old Cathedral. Her dad had told her of how it had been bombed in the Second World War. Somehow, the falling bombs had failed to destroy its spire. She stared up at it now — so beautiful against the blue sky. The fact that it hadn't been destroyed in the war made her frown, made her head hurt because she knew why...

But whatever snippet of history she had read about refused to reveal itself and she remained gazing in awe at a spire that had stood for almost a thousand years. She could almost imagine a ribbon, stretching from those distant days to now, linking the past to the present.

"Buy a pretty ribbon, dear."

The costumed character stood on the corner, a wooden tray balanced around her neck, filled with coiled ribbons. She was red-faced and plump dressed in grubby medieval clothes and mop cap. She held out a blue ribbon. "This will look nice in your pretty fair hair, m'dear. Go on, buy a ribbon."

Megan glanced back for Freya who was nowhere to be seen. "Sorry, I don't wear ribbons. Nobody wears ribbons unless you're a two-year-old."

The woman who had even discoloured her teeth to make herself look authentic insisted. "Ah, show an old woman a kindness, m'dear. I've a family of nine to feed."

Megan groaned, realising she wasn't going to escape without buying something. "How much are they, then?"

"Whatever you think, m'dear."

She fished a twenty pence piece from her purse. "Is this enough?"

The woman put the coin between her teeth and bit down on it. Then, smiling a broken smile, handed Megan a length of ribbon. "God bless you."

Megan took it, pulling a face. "Well, I haven't a clue what I'm going to do with it, but thanks. Oh, and I think your costume looks very realistic — love the teeth!"

Slipping the ribbon into her pocket she strolled on, keeping a look out for more costumed actors.

"Megan!"

She turned at the sound of Freya's voice. Her friend was walking towards her, carefully holding something in two hands — her mobile phone. Megan knew it was just her mobile phone, yet why, for one split-second did it look as if Freya was very carefully walking along, holding a vase, being careful not to spill a drop of its water?

Hurry Ruth... please hurry... A desperate cry echoed through Megan's head and with it, came a dreadful feeling of fear.

The moment passed. Freya slid her mobile into her pocket and caught her up. "There you are! I thought I'd lost you."

Megan felt light headed; her brain was spinning. Why oh why had she imagined her new friend had been carrying a vase of water and that her name was Ruth? And those words — she'd uttered them at some time, or thought them....

Hurry Ruth... please hurry... And with the words, that awful feeling of fear. But that wasn't all. For a brief moment, Freya's short fair hair had been waist length, with a blue ribbon threaded through it. And she hadn't been wearing jeans and sweatshirt at all. She'd been in a blue dress that reached down to her ankles.

Like someone from medieval times.

Chapter Five
A Stolen Cross

North West coast of England 968 A.D.

He wore the tunic of the Aes Dana tribe, keeping their memories alive with his stories as he travelled. The rest of the tribe were long dead now leaving him, as the most cunning, to travel the length and breadth of his native land, seeing all there was to see, taking what he needed, when he needed. No one could stop him. He was immortal.

He touched the Cross of Aes Dana that hung around his neck beneath his tunic. Its power bore through him. Each day he felt its glow like a fire that fed his body, healing any wounds faster than they could bleed. Many who had seen the magic had run screaming away, terrified of such sorcery.

He had laughed as they fled.

Today, disembarking from the ship that had brought him across the Irish Sea to England he felt groggy. It was mere seasickness, nothing fatal. He grinned at the thought. Nothing was fatal now he wore the Cross.

The shipping port of Liverpool abounded with men and

horses and wagons. It stank of fish and ale and foulness of the
filthy streets. He was eager to leave the chaos behind and find
the green countryside he had heard so much about. There
were kingdoms to be won here, and he was ready to do battle
for land, riches, and fair ladies. He was invincible. Even if a
lance speared his heart, he would mend. The power of this
small cross remained as true today as it did one hundred years
ago.

Night was drawing in, and he picked his way through
dark alleyways, side-stepping the drunkards who spilled from
ale houses. But then rough hands grabbed him, began ripping
at his belongings throwing him to the ground. He waited
fearlessly for the killer blow — the dagger or the club.

"He ain't carryin' much for a traveller," the robber named
Carter snarled, holding a dagger close to his throat. "Where's
your purse, where's your gold? Speak up or I'll slit your throat
from ear t' ear."

Carter's eyes lit up as he saw the small gem-stoned
encrusted cross around the traveller's neck. In a second the
robber had sliced through the chain releasing the cross, but the
screech that wailed out from his victim's mouth sent him
reeling. Never had he heard anyone scream like that.

"I didn't touch him!" He defended himself, backing
away, horrified as the traveller tried desperately to scramble to
his feet, crawling towards him on hands and knees, his hand
reaching out, his face pleading.

"The cross... the Cross of Aes Dana. In the name of the
Holy Temple... please... you don't understand... give it
back... Please..."

Carter could only stare. Something was happening to the
traveller. He could have sworn he was no more than forty, but
looking at him now, he looked much older.

There were wrinkles gathering around his face, his
movements were stiffening, as if it had been an old man he'd
just robbed.

He backed off, keeping just a few steps ahead of the old man who continued dragging himself towards him, still pleading for this old metal cross. Then suddenly he stopped crawling and slumped, face down into the mud.

Carter looked helplessly at his accomplices. "I didn't touch him. Curses on me head if I laid a finger on 'im."

"Is 'e dead?" another asked.

"Turn 'im over. See if he's breathin'."

The third man put his boot under the traveller and rolled him over. He screeched like a banshee as a white boned skull stared blindly up at him.

He wasn't just dead, but dead and rotted.

Chapter Six
A Dark World

Freya caught up with Megan. "Sorry about that. It was my mum. She wants me to pick up a library book. She's into…" her voice trailed away. Megan had that stricken look on her face again, like that first day in class. "What's up? You look sort of weird and worried."

"Do I? No, I'm fine. I was just miles away, imagining life in medieval times."

"Are you sure?" Freya pressed, convinced that something was bugging her friend.

"Yeah," Megan shrugged, smiling at her. "No probs."

Freya let it go. Megan had a habit of looking vague at times. Probably she had a lot on her mind — what with moving and everything. Cheerfully she remarked, "I wouldn't have fancied living in those days. No music, no cinemas, no shops, no chocolate!"

"No mobile phones, no telly," Megan added, still smiling. "But it's good around here, the way they make it really olde worlde."

"Do they?" Freya shrugged, wondering what she meant.

She hadn't noticed anything olde worlde in particular.

"Yes, that ribbon seller looked so real."

Freya glanced around. "Oh! I didn't see her. But we do actually have our own modern day Lady Godiva. Her name's Pru and she dresses up and visits schools doing talks and stuff."

"Maybe that was her."

"Could have been," Freya agreed.

Reaching the old cathedral's walls, they stopped and gazed upwards. The old cathedral spire with its turreted balcony seemed to pierce the white clouds.

"Fancy going up?" Freya asked, surprised then to feel her friend shudder so hard her shoulders shook. She frowned at her. Megan was still staring upwards to the top of the spire.

"I... I don't know. Are you allowed up?"

"Oh yes, it'll probably cost a couple of quid." She glanced anxiously at Megan again. "Don't you like heights?"

She remained staring upwards. "I'm okay with them."

Freya saw that the colour had drained from her friend's face. She guessed Megan did have a problem with heights. "Actually, there's about three million steps — I don't know if my legs are up to it. Shall we have a wander around the cathedrals at ground level instead?"

"Yeah, okay, whatever," Megan agreed as if she didn't care one way or the other, but Freya saw how she rubbed her hands down her jeans as if her palms were sweating.

Freya led the way into the old cathedral ruins. It was just a shell — barren sandstone walls, huge glassless windows, except for a few stained-glass panels that had escaped the devastation of the war. A clear blue sky was its roof and where the altar should have been, was a simple charred cross.

Megan seemed dumbstruck. She stood motionless, staring around at the emptiness of it all.

"That's not the real cross," Freya told her. "After the bombings, two roof timbers fell like that, in the shape of a cross."

"It would have had a beautiful ornate ceiling," murmured Megan, sounding a million miles away. "And wooden pews all down here. There'd be holy paintings on the walls, and statues, and candles."

"I know. It's sad, isn't it?" agreed Freya, realising that she'd never really thought of it as once being a proper church. It had always been just a ruin to her. "We did a project in year six about the war and the Blitz. The cathedral had a wooden roof. Loads of incendiary bombs fell on it making it catch fire. The fire brigade couldn't get enough water to put it out, so it just burned to the ground."

She had the feeling that Megan wasn't really listening. She hoped she wasn't boring her. "Fancy looking around the new cathedral now? It's really modern but not everyone likes the style."

"Yes, okay," Megan agreed. "I'd like to see the priory too, the one Godgifu — Godiva — whatever her name was, built."

"Oh that's long gone. Archaeologists unearthed little bits of it but there's not much to see," Freya explained as they walked from the ruins into the immense new cathedral. She turned to Megan, her voice hushed. "So what do you think?"

****

I think I'm going insane! is what Megan thought. Her head was swimming. Nothing made sense. How could the priory be gone? She could even imagine what it looked like from above — looking down on it, which was impossible.

But that wasn't the half of it. As they'd walked around the old cathedral ruins, she had been able to picture how it used to look. She remembered the big black bible that the priest preached from, and the woven cushions you could kneel on, and the monks from the priory who drifted in and out. And when Freya had suggested they go up the spire, she had felt such an overwhelming feeling of panic that she had broken out in a cold sweat.

She'd imagined herself running breathlessly up a narrow spiral stone staircase, feeling the cold damp stone against the palm of her hand as she felt her way upwards. And she was carrying something — something heavy, clutching it fiercely, her heart thudding as if the devil himself was on her tail.

"Okay, marks out of ten," Freya whispered.

It didn't make sense. Nothing made any sense.

Freya was staring at her. "Well, are you totally knocked out by it, or do you hate it?"

Megan was barely aware of it. What was happening to her? Panic welled up in her chest.

"Megan, are you okay?"

"Yes, course," she gulped, trying to stay calm. "It's just… well… amazing!"

"Personally I find it too spiky," Freya said softly as they walked on. "The windows are pretty spectacular though."

"Yes." Megan breathed, her head spinning. "They're lovely…"

****

Dead eyes peered out from the black coils of mist, glimpsing figures, colours, movements. He watched for the susceptible, the ones who shivered and paled as they walked near to his spirit form. His delight then was to wrap his evil stench about them so that they shuddered and grew fearful.

He had been watching, waiting, his head bowed and his hands clasped in prayer, even though prayers no longer fell from his lips for his spirit was black and damned. Then he saw her… her!

The solitary thread of hope that he had clung to these 800 years became a rope — a strong thick rope that he could use to haul himself up from the depth of this purgatory.

His desires grew blacker, his hatred and anger for this mortal child filled his spirit to the brim and he mustered all his energies into the effects of the arched shadowy doorway through which he could pass and merge with the living world for a brief time. But this was his chance and there was one thing he burned to know — and she had the answer.

He swarmed around the unsuspecting mortal, dragging his own personal hell of these bleak corridors with him. His face was inches from hers, his voice a rasp, coaxed from the depth of his damned spirit form that had long since breathed air or tasted water...

****

Megan was studying the panels of mosaic windows that sent a kaleidoscope of colours onto the stone floor. Then everything dimmed. She hadn't seen it coming. One second she was in the vast echoing new cathedral, surrounded by tourists, when suddenly the walls closed in around her and she was alone.

The smell of incense hung heavily in the darkness. Lighted torches standing in niches in the brickwork sent flickering shadows across the rugged flagstones. The stone beneath her feet was rough and uneven. Narrow, arched doorways were set along the passageway and from a darkened recess she felt the claustrophobic presence of a tall shrouded black figure. The evil was tangible, the air chilled and a feeling of nausea swamped her.

A voice, harsh and demonic whispered in her ear.

"Where did you hide it?"

Chapter Seven
Haunted

Megan was a long time getting to sleep that night. Her thoughts were a jumble of images and sounds — Freya carrying a vase and dressed like a medieval little child called Ruth. Knowing how the ruined cathedral once looked and that horrible feeling of being chased up a spiral staircase. But worst of all was the sensation of something evil swamping her, asking where she'd hidden something.

She tossed and turned in her bed, wishing she were back in her old bedroom. Everything felt strange and uncomfortable here.

Finally she slept, falling into a deep dreamless sleep. But in the middle of the night, she awoke with a start, positive that someone was bending over her, whispering to her.

She sat bolt upright in her bed, the words still ringing in her ears.

"Where did you hide it?"

Standing in front of the mirror the next morning, the face that reflected back was tense and pale. There were shadows under her eyes and her hair looked in desperate need of tying back. With a sigh, she felt in her jeans pocket for a hair bobble. Instead she pulled out a deep blue ribbon.

Megan stared at it in dismay, wishing it had a label saying 'Made in Taiwan' on it. But it looked to be made of silk — less than perfect, handmade.

Ancient.

With a cry, she crumpled it up and threw it towards her rubbish bin. It floated to the floor, landing at her feet in the shape of a question mark.

She already knew the question.

Then almost as if she'd conjured up the voice in her head, she heard a murmur in her ear, and that horrible cold cloying sensation wrapped itself around her again so intensely that she shuddered violently.

"Where did you hide it?"

"Who's that?" she cried, spinning round.

Silence surrounded her. But the feeling that she was not alone in her room was so tangible that she almost screamed. She flew downstairs.

"My room is haunted!" she shouted, dashing through to the kitchen.

Her dad peered over the rim of his cup. "And a good morning to you too!"

"I'm not joking. I heard a voice. It asked me where I hid it."

"Hid what, dear?" asked her mum.

Megan threw her hands up. "I don't know! The point is I heard a voice, and it was the same yesterday — some spooky voice in my ear asking where I hid it!"

Her mum took some juice from the fridge. "How peculiar. Do you want some juice? And I'm doing eggs and bacon in a minute."

"Mother! I've just told you I'm being haunted, and you're talking about breakfast. This house is haunted!"

"So what do you suggest?" her mum snapped, slamming

the juice carton on the table. "Get an exorcist in? Do you happen to know a good one?"

"Chill! The both of you," her dad interrupted. "Megan, the house isn't haunted, you're not being haunted. Your room feels strange because everything is new and different. Everything will be okay, once you get used to it."

She stared at them both. "So that's it? I tell you I'm hearing voices, and you tell me I'll get used to it. Great!"

"You must have dreamed it," suggested her mum.

"Mum, I was up, washed and dressed, so unless I was sleep walking, I wasn't dreaming it. I heard a voice and I felt a... a presence, all cold and clammy." She shuddered at the thought of it.

Her parents exchanged glances then her dad got up from his chair. "Want me to check your room?"

Megan nodded, and then followed him upstairs. Her room felt normal.

"Your window is open, it could have been someone walking past outside, talking," he suggested.

It wasn't, and she was wasting her breath. She needed to get some fresh air. "I'm going for a walk. I'll see you later."

"Well, try and be in a better mood when you get back."

She was glad to get out. It would be different if they were experiencing all these weird happenings. Seeing things, hearing things, remembering things. Maybe she was going mad. Maybe all the stress of leaving her life behind was making her slightly crazy. Maybe she was cracking up!

A fresh breeze blew her hair across her face as she followed a little pathway over the stream. It wound its way across the common and then forked in opposite directions. Megan took the route that was more densely wooded. She walked on, going over in her head all the strange things that had happened since arriving here. Suddenly, from nowhere a little dog came bounding towards her, making her jump.

Two seconds later a lanky youth in jeans and a black

hooded top stepped right into her path, barring her way. For a second the sun blinded her to his face and a feeling of absolute terror ran through her veins.

Then she saw the face and her heart continued racing for another reason. "Jamie?"

"Hi! Thought it was you. Me and Sally spotted you way back, we took a short cut across the field. Didn't mean to startle you."

Sally seemed intent on trying to catch a bee, but she paused in her task to allow Megan to fuss her.

"It's not a great idea to jump out of the bushes at girls, you know."

"Suppose not, sorry."

She smiled glad he was there. "It's okay. I like your dog, she's really cute."

"Yeah, she is. So, what are you up to then?"

She wanted to tell him; only he might think her weird if she admitted to being haunted, so she just shrugged. "Nothing much, just taking a walk, exploring a bit, seeing what's here." She strolled on with Jamie loping alongside her and Sally diving in and out of the long grass, chasing anything that moved.

"So how did your day in town go yesterday?"

The myriad of images and emotions ran through her head again. "Er... it was different."

"Did you explore the ancient bits?"

"Some."

Jamie had a ball on a rope and threw it for Sally, sending it flying into the thicket. "See any ghosts?"

Her reply came out as a splutter. "Pardon?"

"See any ghosts? The old parts of the city are crawling with ghosts," he said matter-of-factly as Sally returned with the ball. "Most of the old buildings have at least one resident spook. Don't look at me like that... it's not just me saying it. It's well documented. Loads of people have reported seeing unexplained phenomena."

She chewed on her lip, wondering whether to tell him. But Freya said he was weird and obviously liked the idea of the supernatural. So guessing he might freak her out even more, she lied blatantly, "Well, I didn't experience anything peculiar."

He narrowed his dark eyes as he studied her. "You surprise me. I thought you were the sensitive type who would pick up on that sort of thing."

She glanced away, her skin glowing under his scrutiny. Maybe she was the sensitive type. Maybe that was half the trouble. She tried to sound flippant. "So you've seen a ghost then?"

"Yeah, a couple of times," he said, sending the ball hurtling into the long grass again. "I once saw a misty shape of a figure that looked like he was wearing a robe and a wig, y'know like a judge. That was in St. Mary's Hall. And then another time I felt this ghostly presence. It just kind of descended on me, like a depressing black coldness. It was pretty horrible."

Megan felt her throat tighten. "Where did that happen?"

"Near the cathedral. I got the feeling that..." He stopped what he was saying. "Ah, doesn't matter."

"What? Tell me!"

He shrugged. "Nah, forget it. I don't want you thinking I'm completely nuts — well not until you know me better, and then you'll realise that I am but you'll like me too much by then to do anything about it."

She already did like him, not that she intended him to know that however. "Go on, risk it. What were you going to say?"

He threw the ball again for Sally. "Well I think that particular spook kind of knew me, that's why it got so close to me... double-checking it was me, sort of."

She frowned at him. "How could it know you?"

"From one of my previous lives, obviously."

Megan stared in amazement at him. "How can you be so cool about it? I'd be totally freaked out if I thought I'd lived before... and died before. If you've lived in the past, then you've also died — and that is really freaky."

"Suppose it is. But I'm not unique. Freya has been reincarnated too. She doesn't believe me, but I've definitely got a memory of her. I've got this one fleeting image in my head. She's about eight and she's talking to me and she's kind of frantic, only I can't make out what she's saying. But it's like she's really panicking. She's tugging on my sleeves. I'm wearing a thick rough woolly robe thing. I'm pretty certain I was a monk."

"And Freya was about eight?" Megan murmured, fascinated. She had looked about eight when she'd imagined her carrying a vase. But another thing he'd said intrigued her — Freya's feelings of being frantic and panicking. She had felt panic-stricken thinking about that spiral stone staircase. It had felt like someone was chasing her. "How did you feel?"

He thought hard for a moment, as if it was something he hadn't considered before. "Actually, pretty anxious myself, like I had something really important to do."

Megan nodded. "So do you think emotions and feelings can transcend time, as well as memories of seeing things and people?"

He gave a lopsided grin. "I couldn't have put it better myself. See, I knew you were the sensitive type."

"So what other lives have you lived then?" Megan asked as Jamie strolled along the pathway beside her, his hands clasped in front of him.

"Well, I know I was around in the Second World War, I have such a strong memory of bombers overhead, I was hiding under the stairs with someone else, don't ask me who."

"How weird..."

He broke off what he was saying as his dog returned

without her ball. "Sally, where's your ball? Go find it, go on. Oh! You useless dog, come on, I'll help you." He headed off in the direction he'd thrown it, with Sally prancing alongside. He glanced back. "She'd never make a sniffer dog!"

Megan laughed, liking him a lot and fascinated by what he was saying, especially about Freya. They'd both thought they'd seen her in some distant medieval time. But if it was true, and Jamie wasn't talking a load of rubbish, then it meant that she had been reincarnated too — and that she'd lived at the same period in the past as Jamie and Freya, which was too ridiculous for words.

Watching him searching through the long grass for the ball, she told herself that there had to be a more normal explanation. As she waited, she felt a slight chill, as if the sun had gone behind a black cloud, yet there was barely a cloud in the sky. She rubbed at her arms as her skin started to feel prickly. She felt quite sickly suddenly too.

Jamie found the ball and sent it flying her way. "Go fetch Sal, and keep your eye on it this time — daft dog! Coming your way, Megan, watch your head!"

The ball landed nearby and Sally came bounding towards her. Suddenly she stopped dead in her tracks and stood rigid, hackles up, ears flattened to her head and her tail down. She began to bark.

An icy sensation made her shudder. "Sally, what's up?"

The little dog bared its teeth and snarled. A defiant brave snarl that sent shivers racing up and down Megan's spine.

Jamie came running back. "Sally no! You mustn't bark. Bad girl!"

Unnerved, Megan stood quite still, realising that Sally wasn't barking directly at her — she was barking to the side of her. Slowly she turned her head, expecting someone to be standing there. Feeling as if someone was standing there. It was a chilling sensation, as if there were a dark menacing presence standing right next to her. But she saw no one.

The little dog continued yapping defiantly; even when Jamie picked her up she wouldn't stop. He looked helplessly at Megan. "I'm sorry! I don't know what's got into her. She never barks at people. Behave Sally! Bad dog!"

"It's not her fault..." she tried to say, but her voice seemed to have dried up and the nauseous feeling was getting worse.

Jamie carried his pet towards Megan, talking softly to her. At the same moment Megan felt as if the black cloud was drifting away. She felt warm again and Sally ceased her barking.

"That's better, you silly dog," Jamie crooned, placing her down. "Now you tell Megan that you're sorry for barking at her like that."

Sally trotted along at his heels, her tail wagging sheepishly, eager now to be fussed by Megan.

She stooped down and stroked her. "She's trembling."

"Yeah, I know. Don't know what's got into her. That was weird, she doesn't bark at people. She only goes crazy like that when she's scared of something. But there was nothing to be scared off — she likes you."

"She must have been looking at a ghost then," Megan uttered, trying to make light of it. But deep in her heart, she wondered...

****

Heading back towards his house a half-mile away, Jamie kept a close eye on his little dog. That was weird her barking at Megan like that. She never barked at people. He strode on, his long legs covering the ground swiftly, watching Sally prancing on ahead through the long feathery grasses and diving under brambles dripping with plump blackberries.

A shivery feeling descended upon him from nowhere. He knew the sensation well. It heralded a glimpse back into one of his past lives.

Suddenly he was gazing down at a small girl. She barely came up to his waist. Her long corn-coloured wavy hair was tangled and blowing across her face as she looked pleadingly up at him.

It was a vision he'd had so many times before. Yet this time it was clearer. He could see he was cloaked in the black robe of a Benedictine monk, it was tied around the waist with a cord, and the little girl was tugging frantically on his sleeves. He couldn't tell if she was trying to drag him somewhere or if she was barring his way.

"What are you trying to tell me, Freya?" Jamie murmured out loud, realising suddenly her name wasn't Freya. It was something else and he tried desperately to recall what it was. But like her words themselves, her name eluded him.

These flashbacks from his past lives crept up on him when he least expected them and this one had been recurring ever since he first set eyes on Freya in primary school.

Oddly though, today it was more vivid, less fogged in mist. He could actually see now that her blue dress had pollen and grass stains down the front, as if she'd been carrying flowers in her skirt, and there was mud around the hem. He'd never noticed that before.

If only he could hear what she was saying to him.

Chapter Eight
Slipping Back

Tell me the secrets behind these red stone bricks,
of your walls so thick
they have withstood a thousand years.
Tell me the secrets behind this majestic steeple
and all the people,
Tell me all their joys and fears.
Tell me the secrets behind stone steps worn smooth
of every crack and groove
that hint at lives that have come and gone.
Tell me the secrets behind this sturdy oak door
and your ancient floor
Tell me of the people who we shall see no more.

"Very good, Megan!" Mrs. Lovejoy praised, nodding appreciatively as she slowly paced around the classroom. "A thought provoking piece of poetry."

Megan's cheeks were burning. She'd felt compelled to write the poem, but hadn't expected to be asked to read it out. "Thank you, miss."

Her teacher remained clearly impressed. "I think what I'm most pleased about Megan, is the fact that you've only just moved to Coventry — what is it now, a week, ten days?

"Eight days, miss."

"Exactly! A very short time, yet our lovely old Cathedral has inspired you to write a poem about it. I think that's very commendable. What does everyone else think?"

Megan was aware of a few nods and murmurs of agreement, although she doubted that anyone was particularly bothered one way or the other, although Freya put her thumbs up.

"Move over, Lord Byron!" she said, smiling. "That was pretty good."

Jamie's hand shot up. "Miss, I've written a poem about our cat."

There were a few giggles.

"I don't mind reading it, miss."

Mrs. Lovejoy cast Megan another nod of encouragement and switched her attention to Jamie. "Stand up then, Jamie, and speak slowly and clearly. I'm sure we're all very keen to hear about your cat."

Jamie stood, cleared his throat a little too enthusiastically, so that most of the girls practically gagged in disgust, and began.

Our little cat is a fat little cat.
He eats and he eats and he eats.
He's a round ball of fluff
But he's ever so tough
And I really like him like that.

He stood there, raising his upturned hands to receive his applause. Everyone consented, even Mrs. Lovejoy.

"Well done, Jamie, I'm delighted you'd made the effort to try your hand at poetry."

"Thank you, miss. It is actually a work of fiction, unlike Megan's masterpiece. I have to admit I don't actually own a cat, I have a dog — but it wouldn't rhyme."

As everyone groaned, he glanced at Megan with a cute grin on his face. Her heart gave a little lurch and the colour rose in her cheeks.

Freya gave her a nudge and whispered, "He fancies you!"

After lunch it was art class. Mr. Montgomery, the art teacher, was setting up a vase of chrysanthemums on his desk for everyone to paint.

"Shouldn't it be sunflowers, sir?" Jamie suggested. "Old what's-his-name, Van Gogh got millions for his painting of sunflowers."

"He didn't get anything," Yvette, who was sitting behind him, remarked, flicking a scrunched up piece of paper at him. "He was dead and buried long before it got auctioned off for millions."

"Make a name for yourself then, Jamie. Create a brilliant masterpiece today and you might be on the road to becoming the next Van Gogh or Michelangelo," suggested Mr. Montgomery, struggling to create an attractive arrangement with the chrysanthemums. He stood back, looking at his efforts in dismay. "As you can see, floristry is not my *forté*. Can any of you girls do a better job of this than me?"

"Isn't that sexist, sir?" enquired Jamie casting Megan a little wink. "Implying that only girls can arrange flowers."

Mr. Montgomery hoisted the chrysanthemums out of the vase and thrust them in Jamie's direction. "It probably is, young man, and we can't have that, can we? Come and see what you can do."

With the rest of the class whistling, Jamie sauntered up to the desk and attempted to arrange them. Messing about, he clumsily tipped the vase over, scattering the flowers all over the floor.

"What an idiot!" Freya groaned. "Come on Megan, let's

get this sorted."

"Sorry, sir!" Jamie wailed.

"Sit down, Jamie," sighed Mr. Montgomery. "Let the girls do it, as I suggested in the first place. Thank you, girls."

Megan flashed a shy smile at Jamie before she and Freya stooped down to gather the flowers up. Fortunately there hadn't been any water in the vase, but all the flowers had fallen in an untidy heap on the classroom floor — a mess of orange petals and green stalks, their fragrance quite strong and heady.

For a second Megan felt dazzled by the bright colours and then she realised it was the sunlight that was dazzling her. It was directly overhead blazing down on her and little Ruth, making her long fair curls shine. And the flowers weren't on the floor at all. They were gathered in colourful heaps in their skirts as they clutched the hems, making baskets for the wild flowers they'd just picked from the meadow. Their colours were brilliant, a profusion of scarlet, pink, violet, and yellow.

"There should be 184," said Megan aware of the melodic tinkle of water rushing over pebbles in the nearby stream.

"I don't think so," puzzled Freya. "Why should there be that many anyway?"

"One for every year of her life," Megan murmured as the warm breeze blew her hair over her eyes.

"Pardon?"

"One for every year of her life," Megan repeated, pushing her hair aside with her arm, aware that her hands were muddy. Her feet, clad in soft canvas shoes were sinking into the mound of freshly dug earth. At one end of the mound a small wooden cross had been pushed hurriedly into the soil.

"Who's life?" Freya asked.

Megan stared at her, puzzled that she could have forgotten so quickly. "Talitha's of course!"

"Who's Talitha?" Freya asked, her voice sharp.

Megan's brown eyes creased. Ruth looked different

suddenly. Her long tumbling curls had gone. Her hair was short and sleek — and she looked older suddenly. Not eight any more — fourteen or fifteen. As old as her!

She barely recognised this girl staring at her with a bewildered look on her face. And the flowers in the hem of her long skirt were gone. Her skirt was grey and short.

"Ruth!" Megan cried out, looking frantically around. There were faces everywhere, and she was surrounded by four walls and a ceiling, she couldn't see the blue sky any more. But worse, where had her little sister vanished to?

And who was this girl, standing where Ruth had stood a second ago?

Panic flared within her. Where was her sister? "Ruth!"

"Megan, what's wrong? Who are you on about? Who's Tailtha? Who's Ruth?" the girl standing beside her demanded, grabbing her arms and giving her a little shake. "Megan, answer me, who are you talking about?"

"Come along girls," someone said. "Stop chattering and get on with it. It'll be home time before we get started at this rate."

Megan's head spun. She stared in a daze at the large orange flowers on their long thick stalks. These weren't the flowers she and her little sister had just picked from the meadow a moment ago. They had gathered poppies and buttercups and forget-me-nots.

These were chrysanthemums! She suddenly realised what they were. Chrysanthemums. And she was in art class. Of course. These flowers were for her art class to draw. Jamie had knocked the lot onto the floor. She was helping to pick them up — helping Freya, her friend, not her little sister...

Not her little sister.

Her eyes began to sting. Her sister was gone. "Ruth!" she sobbed as hot tears welled up in her eyes and streamed uncontrollably down her cheeks.

Her knees buckled and she clung onto the edge of a desk

as the floor rushed up to meet her. Jamie caught her before it did.

As a black cloud engulfed her, Megan realised with a flood of grief that she didn't have a little sister.

Not any more...

Chapter Nine
Rumours of Magic

Middle England 1028 A.D.

"Is that the fellow?" Ralph, second cousin to the Earl of Ansty whispered to his accomplice.

The other man, Thomas, crouching low behind an oak tree, risked another look at the young bearded man sleeping beside a campfire. His snoring and the empty liquor flagon dangling from his limp hand told them that he would not be putting up a fight.

"I'd say so," Thomas replied softly. "He fits the description well and rumour has it that he was heading this way. I can't see if he's wearing it though."

"No, nor I," murmured Ralph. "Be prepared. I'll tread closer and try to see."

As Ralph moved silently and stealthily towards the drunken sleeper, Thomas drew his sword in readiness. They'd had their orders. The Earl desired a certain cross known as the Cross of Aes Dana, which supposedly held magical powers of sorts. Rumour had it that it was being worn by a common robber thought to be in the Mercia area.

Ralph crept forward, his step light. He looked down at the young man whose mouth sagged open and whose snores sounded like the grunting of a pig. His jerkin was open slightly at the neck and Ralph could see a leather thong that no doubt bore some kind of pendant next to his skin.

He glanced back at Thomas who stood prepared to lunge with his blade if the man awoke and went for his own sword. Ralph indicated that there was indeed a pendant and that he was going to try and see what it was.

As his hand reached down, the drunk bellowed out a rasping snore, making Ralph jump back for a second. As the man's breathing settled down once more Ralph tried again. His fingers closed around the narrow strip of leather. He felt the heat from the sleeping man's skin and smelled the foul stench of his breath. Gently, he released the pendant from beneath his jerkin.

Leaning over the sleeping man, with the pendant in the palm of his hand, Ralph thought he wouldn't give a brass farthing for such an ugly object. It was a dull iron cross, encrusted with gemstones of various colours. His lip curled in disdain, he had expected the mysterious Cross of Aes Dana to have glowed like gold. This was dull and blackened with age and sweat.

Nevertheless, it was possible that it was the cross he'd been ordered to find, and for which the Earl had promised a tidy reward. All he had to do now was run his dagger across the leather strap and slip the cross off.

The young fool was so drunk it was a simple task.

He smiled broadly at Thomas, and clutching the Cross of Aes Dana firmly in his hand he strode back to his accomplice, leaving the drunk none the wiser.

Thomas clapped him warmly on the back and together they swaggered back to where they had left their horses. The Earl would be well pleased.

****

In his drunken sleep Carter dreamed of the night he had robbed a traveller of a gemstoned cross. The nightmare had haunted him for the last sixty years. Asleep or awake he'd never been able to forget how the man had crawled on hands and knees begging for the cross to be given back to him. Etched into his brain too was how the man had aged, died, and rotted away before his very eyes.

Carter groaned in his sleep, everything ached, his bones felt stiff and his joints seemed to be seizing up. He opened one eye and through his drunken stupor he saw a liquor flagon fall from his hand. Only it couldn't be his hand. His hands were young and supple. He hadn't aged a day since he slipped that stolen cross around his own neck. But the hand he was squinting at now through ale-blurred eyes was an old man's hand. Scrawny, arthritic, smothered in brown age spots. Vaguely as his eyes closed again, he wondered whose hand it could be.

Chapter Ten
Secrets

Freya was desperate for school to be over. She was worried sick about Megan. The Head had sent for Megan's mum to come and pick her up and take her home. The afternoon had seemed endless after she'd gone.

As soon as the home bell sounded, Freya was away, finding her way to Megan's house. Anxiously she pressed the doorbell and waited. Megan's mum answered it; she looked stressed.

"Hello! I'm Freya Mason, a friend of Megan's. How is she?"

"Freya? Ah, you're the one who reminds her of someone."

"Am I?"

"So it seems," Mrs. Miller said, inviting her in. "Nice to meet you Freya. It's very kind of you to call around."

"I just wanted to check she's okay," Freya said, following her through to the living room.

Megan was lying on the sofa, clutching her mobile phone, looking a healthier colour than the deathly white shade she had turned just before collapsing.

"Hey! That was some spectacular performance this afternoon," Freya exclaimed skipping over to her. "I don't know! The lengths some people will go to, to get out of maths." She sat down beside her. "How are you feeling now?"

"I'm okay," Megan replied, but Freya heard the catch in her voice, and instantly knew that she wasn't okay at all.

Mrs. Miller hovered nearby. "I wish I'd registered with a doctor — I've had so much to think about, it completely slipped my mind."

"Mum, I'm absolutely fine. I just got up a bit quick and the blood rushed to my head. I went a bit dizzy. I didn't actually faint."

Mrs. Miller looked to Freya for confirmation. "Is that right?"

"I've told you, mum," Megan interrupted before Freya could answer. "Stop fretting. I'm okay."

"I can't help fretting, I'm your mother!"

Freya tried to catch her friend's eye, as if to say 'mothers — they're always worrying about something!' But Megan turned away, refusing to meet her gaze, as if she had something to hide — some dark secret. Freya's stomach tightened and she felt quite hurt that Megan was shutting her out too.

She glanced at her friend again, hoping that she had misinterpreted her body language a moment ago. But once again Megan avoided her gaze and stared blindly at some program on the television.

Freya felt her throat ache.

Mrs. Miller heaved a sigh. "Would either of you like a glass of orange?"

"If you like," Megan murmured, still staring at the TV screen.

"I'd love one, thank you," said Freya, then waited until Mrs. Miller had gone through to the kitchen before softly asking, "Megan, what's wrong. Why won't you tell me?"

"There's nothing to tell. Can we drop the subject please? I just went a bit woozy, that's all."

"Megan, you were more than just woozy, the things you were saying before you fainted just didn't make sense. Please, tell me. Something is really stressing you out. I can see it in your face. And who are Talitha and Ruth?"

"No-one! I was just thinking of someone else, that's all. It's no big deal." She turned her attention back to the television, cutting Freya out again.

"You can tell me," Freya whispered, touching Megan's hand. She was shocked to see tears well up suddenly in her friend's eyes.

Mrs. Miller returned then with orange juice and biscuits. Freya jumped to her feet so she couldn't see her daughter in tears. "Mmm, I love these choccy biscuits. Thank you." Behind her, she sensed Megan getting up off the sofa.

"Will you bring them upstairs, Freya?" Megan called back from halfway out of the door. "Telly's rubbish. May as well put some music on."

Mrs. Miller looked relieved that her daughter was doing something normal. But as Freya went to follow, she said softly, "Keep an eye on her. I've never known her to faint before."

Up in her room, Megan browsed through her CD collection, chatting on about various artists, avoiding Freya's enquiring looks at all costs.

Finally, Freya couldn't bear it any longer. "Megan will you pack this in and tell me what's bugging you?"

"Nothing's bugging me," Megan answered, but her eyes fluttered shut and she turned her head aside.

"I'm not stupid. Something is worrying you. And who's this Talitha person... the one that's one hundred and eighty-four years old? A flower for every year of her life, you said. Megan, it was like you were in another world for a few moments today."

Megan took a deep breath and picked out another CD. "Have you heard this albu—"

"Please, talk to me!" cried Freya.

"There's nothing to talk about!" Megan snapped back.

"Don't cut me out like this," Freya pleaded, feeling close to tears herself now. "I'm your friend. I know we haven't known each other long but..."

Megan made a kind of pained whimpering sound and then slumped down on her bed, burying her face in her pillow.

Freya sat down beside her; she spoke softly. "I know you must miss your real friends, but I'm a mate too, only I can't help you unless you tell me what's wrong."

Megan remained buried in her pillow.

"Please!" Freya begged.

Quietly then, her voice muffled, Megan murmured, "You'll think I'm crazy."

"No I won't, I promise."

"Well you should!" Megan said raggedly, sitting up and hugging her knees to herself. "I think I'm crazy. I keep..." Her voice trailed away.

"What? Tell me!" Freya exclaimed, not knowing what to think — except that her new friend was in a bad way over something.

Megan finally looked up, her eyes brimming with tears. "I... I keep imagining things and hearing things, and I know stuff that I shouldn't know, and I think that you were..." she stopped in mid-sentence, pressing her fingertips over her eyes.

Freya said nothing. She sat quietly, waiting patiently for her to continue. When Megan spoke again, it was to talk about what happened at school that day. Freya listened without interrupting, so relieved that finally Megan was opening up to her and telling her what was wrong.

"In art class today," Megan began slowly. "One minute I was picking up the flowers that Jamie spilled when suddenly everything changed. The classroom vanished, everybody in it vanished, except..."

Freya waited, seeing a whole mixture of conflicting expressions flash across her friend's face. "Except?"

"Except me and... and someone else..." She paused briefly before continuing, "We'd been collecting flowers for a grave. There was mud on my hands, and I'd got stupid little canvas shoes that fastened with a button, and my hair was much longer and blowing across my eyes. There was a little hand-made cross, two bits of wood tied with string — that was the headstone on a mound of earth. And we'd picked the flowers from the meadow, all 184 of them for Talitha because she was 184 years old and she'd just died! There!" Her eyes shone with tears. "Stupid or what?"

Freya couldn't speak. She didn't know what to say. All she could think of doing was wrapping her arms around Megan and giving her a hug. Eventually she asked, "And who is Talitha?"

Megan's face crumpled. "I don't know. I honestly and truthfully don't know. If I knew I would tell you."

"And what about the other person — Ruth?"

Megan turned to stare blindly at some speck in the distance. "My little sister..."

Freya looked sadly at her. "No wonder you fainted."

"I'm going insane, aren't I?"

"No you're not," Freya stated. "We'll get to the bottom of all this. We'll work it out. We will. I promise!"

"But what if I am going mad? What if I'm schizophrenic?"

"Then we get you some medical help," Freya said, not expecting the tears to well up in Megan's eyes again. But this time it was tears of relief.

"Thank you," Megan breathed. "I was terrified that you'd run screaming for the door thinking I was some mad girl."

"Yes, well I've always thought that!" Freya joked, glad to see her friend actually smiling again. "That's better. Right!

Now, what I think we need to do first is drink this juice because I'm dying of thirst and we eat these biscuits, because they're chocolate!"

Megan blew her nose then smiled tearfully. "Good plan so far."

"Precisely, and then you can start telling me about all these weird things that have been happening since... well, since when?

"Since moving here, actually," said Megan. "I felt like I was coming home..."

Freya sat cross-legged on the bed listening, fascinated as Megan told her about the flashes of memories she'd been having. In a way it reminded her of Jamie's weird ramblings. But she listened, intrigued as Megan told her about the face that had drifted into her head from nowhere, and how she could visualise the cathedral before it was bombed. She sat amazed as Megan described running frantically up a spiral stone staircase. And she'd shuddered as Megan spoke of being haunted and someone whispering in her ear about hiding something.

Heading home later, Freya felt so sorry for her new friend. Was it possible that Megan had lived before? Or was she suffering some mental problem?

But then something else occurred to her. Despite everything that Megan had told her tonight, Freya still had a vague feeling that it wasn't everything. She sensed that Megan was still keeping some secret from her.

It worried her to think how bad that secret must be.

****

Megan had trouble falling asleep again that night. She lay staring at the ceiling, a bedside lamp bathing her room in a soft pink glow. Her thoughts were spinning crazily. Had she really lived before? Could her new friend really be her little sister from a past life?

It was just so insane. Reincarnation wasn't real — it was a myth, surely. Yet it would explain why she had been so drawn towards Freya and all the other feelings of *déjà vu*. It didn't explain the ghostly voice in her head though, nor the horrible sensation of being haunted.

Shuddering, she drew the duvet up around her neck. She was glad that Freya had dragged the truth out of her — although she'd kept quiet about them being sisters. That might really have freaked Freya out.

As sleep took over, Megan tried to let her mind drift, to let the memories flow back. If she could only make sense of all this, she would be glad to remember everything. But nothing became any clearer. Eventually as she was drifting halfway between sleep and semi-consciousness the image of a face formed in her mind — a woman's face — like before.

She looked about thirty with dark brown plaited hair. Her eyes sparkled at first as she mouthed incoherent words, but then dimmed, and became wreathed in sadness as she faded away.

Megan tried to call her back, to ask what she had said. She couldn't make out the words. It was so far back… so long ago.

Tossing and turning, murmuring in her sleep, Megan rolled over and slept deeply. The face drifted back, closer, as if she were leaning over Megan as she slept. And then she pressed something into Megan's hand before fading away.

Megan felt the warm angular metal of a cross against her skin, and smooth gemstones set within the iron, and the thin chain that enabled it to be worn around the neck.

In her sleep Megan's fingers touched the pouch she wore around her own throat. It contained a fusion of herbs to keep away the plague — at least that's what the elders said, and who was she to argue?

Her fingers tightened around the object in her hand. The

cross was heavy, made of iron — a burden in so many ways…

She slept on unconsciously checking the cross was still there throughout the night, clasping it tightly in her hand.

Only as she started to wake did she feel it slipping away. Desperately she tried to hang onto it but as consciousness took over, so the cross slipped back into the unreal world of her dreams.

Her bedside lamp was still on and she uncoiled her clenched hand and stared at it, half expecting to see the imprint of the cross in her skin.

But there was nothing. Just marks of her fingernails in her palms. She felt for the pouch of herbs around her throat. But of course they, like the cross were simply the imaginations of a dream.

Or fragmented memories of a life she had lived long, long ago.

****

She told Freya. At first break they dawdled around the playground, arms linked, trying to work out what it all meant.

"And what are you pair plotting?" Jamie asked, swooping down on them like some big bird of prey, wrapping his arms around them both and poking his head in between theirs.

"Nothing that concerns you," Freya informed him haughtily.

He smelt of minty chewing gum and had an impish grin that Megan found irresistible.

"That's better!" Jamie said, turning his head to look at her. "That's the first time you've smiled all morning."

"So you've had nothing better to do all morning than watch me?" she asked, secretly pleased.

"Absolutely! You interest me… I sense hidden depths."

She glanced at Freya. "Do you really?"

"Yes indeed. And I'm getting clearer fragmented splinters of flashback memories since you've been around, Megan Miller, which tells me that we have a link. Only I can't fathom it out any deeper... yet!"

Freya's dark eyes glinted with mischief. "Was she one of your Viking conquests, when you came pillaging through Britain back in the day?"

"Help! I hope not!" Megan wailed in mock horror, blushing crimson.

"No, I'd have remembered," Jamie said, wiggling his eyebrows in Megan's direction deepening her blush. "But seriously folks, I sense our link is from the time when I'm wearing a monk's robe. It's a black heavy robe, tied around the middle with a cord. The Benedictine monks at Godiva's priory wore black robes, so that would tie in. It's got a hood..."

"So you wore a hoody even in those days!" Freya exclaimed, making both girls burst out laughing.

Jamie glanced disdainfully from Freya to Megan. "This girl never takes me seriously."

"Go on Jamie, we're listening, honestly," Megan promised, keeping her voice light, while deep down she was hanging onto his every word. If his memories were linked with hers it might help her understand.

He strolled along between the two of them, his hands clasped in front of him in that characteristic way of his. "As I was saying, it's during that period of history when I was a Benedictine monk."

"You're positive about that now?" Freya teased.

"The evidence points that way. And. I've got the name Henry in my head, Henry after the King. But most importantly is that I'm with Freya here." He jerked his head in her direction. "She was ranting on about something even then."

"So you've told me many times!" Freya groaned. "Haven't you figured out what I'm saying? I'd really like to know."

Although Megan knew her friend was being flippant, she held her breath desperate to hear more.

Jamie's expression changed, a far-away look came over him. "We're in a village I think, it's very woody and it's early evening — hey, I've never realised that before." He glanced at Megan. "Since you've been around, Megan Miller, I'm getting more and more vivid memories."

Her heartbeat quickened. "What else can you see?"

Freya rolled her eyes heavenwards. "Oh, don't encourage him."

"The sun is just going down," Jamie continued, gazing over their heads. "The sky is a brilliant red, and Freya here is all uptight about something. You're quite small — smaller than you are now and that's hard to imagine, isn't it."

"Just because you're lanky," Freya said defensively.

"Your hair is right down to your waist, it's all wavy and half tied back in a blue ribbon. You ought to grow it like that again, you know."

"Get on with it!" Freya moaned.

"Okay, right, you've got a blue dress on, and I get the feeling that someone has died and you're really frantic about something... But that's about it."

Somehow, Megan kept walking. But the playground had become a blur and her head was spinning crazily.

Someone blew a whistle — the teacher, telling everyone it was time to go back to class. They headed back into the building. Megan was vaguely aware that Jamie was still talking, but she couldn't decipher his words. All she could think of was that he'd described Freya — or Ruth — perfectly, right down to the colour of her dress. And if two people shared the same memory, then it had to be real. Didn't it?

****

Freya followed the other kids back into class, deep in

thought. Up until now she'd always thought that Jamie talked a load of rubbish, but now she wasn't so sure. Someone had died in Megan's flashback. She'd put flowers on a grave — one for every year of her life, that's what Megan had said. One for every year of Talitha's life — whoever Talitha was.

She glanced across the classroom to Jamie, as always he'd got a crowd around him, always with an audience to listen to his stories, always the centre of attention. She couldn't help wondering… maybe he'd overheard Megan yesterday, talking about a grave just before she fainted. Maybe he'd just pinched that snippet to give his own stories more impact.

She watched him making the little crowd around him laugh. He was never short of something to say. Her eyes narrowed; she wouldn't put it past him to have made that story up to hook Megan.

She glanced across at her friend, sitting quietly at her desk. She'd looked shocked when Jamie had mentioned that someone had died. What would she be thinking now?

****

Freya sat down next to Megan and gave her a nudge, startling Megan from her daydream. "I reckon he made that up!"

Megan said nothing, but she had that 'stricken' look on her face again.

"It was a trick," Freya hissed, keeping one eye on Jamie. He had the knack of creeping up behind you unexpectedly, always catching bits of private conversations. "He must have overheard you yesterday and decided to weave it into his own little fairy tale."

Megan looked utterly miserable. "He wouldn't do that, would he?"

"Of course he did…" Freya clammed up as Jamie headed their way.

He paused beside Megan's desk. "By the way, I'm sorry about Sally's behaviour on Sunday. There was no doggy treat for her when we got home, that's for sure."

"Something obviously scared her. Is she okay now?"

"Yeah, fine. I meant to apologise to you yesterday, only I forgot when you did your dying fly impersonation. You okay now?"

Megan barely looked at him. "Yes, I'm okay. Thanks."

As soon as Jamie had gone, Freya hissed, "What's this about his dog?"

"Oh, she went a bit peculiar with me. She was fine to begin with, then she got all freaked out and wouldn't come anywhere near me."

"Weird owner, weird dog," Freya said under her breath. "So what happened exactly?"

Megan shrugged. "Well, she just stood there barking and growling — not exactly at me, more to my side, like there was someone standing there…"

Freya felt a shiver run down her spine. "Megan! You didn't mention that yesterday!"

"Didn't I? I've told my parents I'm being haunted. They think I'm imagining things."

"It must all be linked with the weird memories you're having," Freya suggested cautiously, not wanting to scare her friend any more than she already was. "Although… you do know that dogs can sense things…"

"Ghosts and stuff?" Megan finished for her.

She nodded. "Maybe it's connected to that woman you keep seeing in your dreams.

Maybe she's the one asking where you hid it — whatever it is."

"No!" Megan exclaimed. "Not Talitha! Talitha was lovely…"

Freya gasped. "Megan! You've just put a name to the face!"

"It just came to me!" Megan gasped. "Her name's Talitha. The face I keep seeing — it's Talitha!"

"And you know she's lovely," Freya added, trying somehow to keep her voice down. "And you know Talitha gave you a metal and gemstone cross when she was about thirty years old. You know she lived till she was 184 and you put flowers on her grave. Help! How old would that have made you?"

Megan stared at her, wide eyed. "Ancient! I should have been ancient, only I wasn't. When I put those flowers on Talitha's grave I was just about the age I am now. It's insane. I'm going insane."

"No you're not! There has to be a logical explanation," Freya promised, giving her friend a little hug. But for the life of her, she couldn't think what that explanation could be.

Chapter Eleven
Survivor by Sorcery

1048 A.D. Mercia, Middle England

The Earl of Ansty stood trembling in the field — the last man standing. All around his feet lay the dead and the dying. A blanket of bodies, men lying in grotesque poses, limbs severed, arrows piercing flesh. The grass blackened with blood. Brave, loyal, and true men who had fought until the bitter end.

Not just his own men but the enemy too — they had battled gallantly. But one by one they had fallen, even the strongest had eventually fallen, fatigued, almost welcoming the final fatal blow.

Now the Earl stood there, his sword hanging limply from his bloodied arm. And as he gazed around at the desperate tragic scene, tears streamed from his eyes.

His right hand opened and his sword fell to the ground at his feet.

Looking down at himself then, he saw the arrows that had pierced his own body and the gashes from swords as the opposing warriors had attempted to slay him.

They could not. Each vicious blow from sword or lance that struck him had sent him reeling, but each time he had got to his feet and fought back. His opponents had crumbled at the sight of a man so badly injured who could fight with such strength and power.

Some had fled realising sorcery was at work. Others had hacked away feverishly, desperate to cut him to ribbons. Yet all they did was to drain their own bodies of strength, and when the moment came, he struck them down easily.

Silence enveloped him now the battle cries had ended and the last clash of metal against metal had ceased. The air was so silent it hurt.

Clutching an arrow shaft half embedded in his chest, the Earl pulled it from his body. The shock of pain and his scream of agony sent the crows screeching into the sky. Almost immediately the pain eased and the gaping wound closed.

One by one, he pulled all the arrows from his body, crying out in agony for the few seconds it took to do the deed.

When the last arrow was cast to the ground, he looked down at himself once again. His tunic, armour, breeches, and even his shoes were sliced to ribbons, yet he knew the flesh beneath did not even bear a scar.

The pain he felt however was far deeper set. Clutching his chest, he felt the small metal cross he wore on a slender chain around his neck - the Cross of Aes Dana. And as his weary eyes gazed wretchedly at the scene of carnage all around him, he fell to his knees and wept bitterly.

****

Two years later

The sight of the magnificent Priory of St. Mary and the spires of Saint Michael's church filled the Earl of Ansty's heart with pride as it always did when he passed this way.

His village of Ansty lay just a few miles outside of the main town and by comparison was merely a hamlet; whereas Couaentree, or Cofa's Tree as some still called it, was a thriving market town and a stopping place for travellers and scholars. It was ruled by Leofric, the Earl of Mercia, and his wife, Godgifu.

The Earl rode his horse across the cobbles to the gateway of the priory and dismounted, hoping and praying he was doing the right thing.

Godgifu welcomed him into her quarters. She served him a goblet of wine, and sat opposite him quietly and serenely as he quenched his thirst.

She wore a gown lavishly embroidered with golden threads and a blue veil edged in stiff white linen that framed her face. Her long fair hair, now streaked with grey, tumbled around her shoulders. The Earl still thought her the most beautiful woman he had ever laid eyes on, even though she was middle-aged now and fine lines creased her pale skin.

She smiled. "My good Earl, what brings you here?"

"I have a gift for your church…" He dropped his head in shame. "No, I cannot lie, it is not a gift but a curse."

A slight flinch of her blue eyes was the only sign of any alarm. "Please explain."

He took the cross from around his neck. He had polished it until it gleamed. "This is the Cross of Aes Dana."

"It looks to be a fine gift for our church, yet you say it's a curse?"

The Earl breathed deeply before explaining — telling as much of its history as he knew and had heard rumoured. He then told of his own experiences and belief that it did indeed hold the power of everlasting life.

She gazed at it, her eyes wise beyond her years. "We will hide it away. In our church we have statues already bedecked with rosaries and crosses and necklaces. This will be lost amongst their splendour. Come."

He followed her into the church. It was empty except for a few monks kneeling in prayer and meditation. Godgifu bid him to fetch a tall stool and then to climb upon it to place the Cross of Aes Dana around the neck of a statue of Saint Osberga.

He was glad to be rid of it. But as he stepped down from the stool, he felt the muscles in his back twinge.

Godgifu took his elbow to steady him. "How many years has the cross been in your possession?"

"Some twenty years," he answered, feeling them rapidly catching up on him.

Godgifu smiled kindly. "That is not so bad. Come, let us sit a while and pray. You still have time for that."

Chapter Twelve
Nightmare

As Megan drifted off to sleep that night she wondered whether she would see Talitha again in her dreams. She almost hoped she would. But the figure that loomed up from her subconscious was something from her worst nightmares.

Something woke her, a noise, or something. Her heart was thudding as she switched on her bedside lamp. The room filled with a dim orange glow that flickered like candlelight.

Lying in her bed, Megan's eyes focused on the wall facing her. There was a shadow on it — the shadow of a tall, thin, arched doorway.

She stared at it, trying to figure out what was casting the shadow, and as she stared it seemed to quiver. At first it was like candlelight was making it shimmer. But then it quite visibly moved, and slowly, very slowly, swung open.

Standing in the black void revealed through this open doorway, she saw the tall shadowy figure of a monk.

Megan couldn't move, couldn't breathe. He was wearing a dark robe tied with a cord and he had a hood. His head was lowered and his hands were clasped in front of him as if in prayer.

Desperately, she tried to scream, tried to jump out of bed, but she was paralysed with shock, unable to make a sound or move a muscle. All she could do was stare as he slowly emerged from the black doorway. Silently, he drifted across her bedroom floor, coming towards her, closer and closer.

She shrank back into her pillows as he reached the side of her bed and loomed over her. Slowly he lowered his head to hers.

She stared upwards. She couldn't make out his face. There was nothing but blackness beneath the hood. But from this black void a bleak voice uttered, "Where did you hide it?"

"I'm not telling you!" Megan shrieked, jerking forward, pushing her face into the black space beneath the cowl. "I'll never tell you! Never!"

Her entire body lurched and her eyes sprang open.

A dream... just a dream!

She wasn't sitting up yelling at some vile apparition. She was curled up on her side, her head in the pillows. Her lamp turned off. Everything was quiet. She hadn't screamed at him, she couldn't have. A scream that loud would surely have brought her parents running.

It was just a dream — a nightmare. She rolled over and reached for the switch on her lamp.

Her room was instantly bathed in a soft pink glow and she fell back onto her pillow, her eyes settling on her bedroom wall opposite...

And the shadow of a tall, thin, arched doorway.

Scrambling frantically from her bed, Megan ran into her parents' room, shaking her mum awake. "Mum! Dad! There's something in my room... wake up!"

"Spiders won't hurt you," her dad mumbled sleepily.

"What's happening?" demanded her mum, sitting up, eyes still half shut.

Megan was trembling. "I told you we were haunted!

There's a ghost. I've seen it. It's a monk and he's vile... he was in my room. He came out of the wall. I know it was a dream, but the doorway is still there."

"Roger, wake up," said her mum, giving her husband a nudge. "Calm down now, Megan, you've just had a bad dream. Oh, you're shaking like a leaf. Roger, go and check will you!"

Muttering and still half asleep, her dad dragged himself out of bed and shuffled through to her bedroom. Megan followed, hanging onto his arm. "What am I looking for?"

She could still see the faint shadow of an arched doorway on her wall. "There! See it?"

Her mum had followed them. "My eyes won't focus. Roger, can you see what she's talking about?"

He walked over to the wall and ran his hand over the shadow. "Well I can see something. I'd say this was an alcove that's been bricked up at some time or other. It hasn't been plastered that well and in a certain light it shows an imprint."

"But in my dream it opened and this horrible black figure drifted out."

Her mum gave her a little hug. "It was just a nightmare, love."

"I'm not imagining it, mum! The ghost of a monk came out of that doorway and bent right over me. It asked me where I hid it."

Her mum pulled her dressing gown around herself, as if she was cold suddenly. "You know, I think we will get you down to the doctor's, you might be suffering from a bit of stress, what with changing schools and everything."

"I'm stressed because I'm being haunted," Megan exclaimed. "Ever since we came here I've had these feelings, and heard voices."

Her mum headed for the bedroom door. "I'm going to make you a mug of warm milk..."

"I don't want warm milk!" Megan screamed.

Her dad turned angrily on her. "Megan! That's enough. Don't shout at your mother, she's only trying to help. You've had a nightmare and you need to calm down."

"It's a bit difficult to calm down when a ghost is roaming around your bedroom."

Her dad gave her a long serious look. "Megan, you're overreacting and over tired. Get yourself back to bed. Leave the light on if you must — and drink that milk when your mother brings it up."

Later, Megan sat bolt upright in bed, gripping the mug of warm milk until it went cold and a film had formed across its surface. She set it aside, her eyes not wavering from the shadow of the arched doorway. She stared at it until exhaustion finally overtook her and she fell into a fitful sleep.

****

Freya listened, fascinated and horrified as Megan told her all about her nightmare. Megan had been waiting at the school gates, and now garbled out the whole tale as they headed into class.

Getting the story straight in her own head, Freya said, "So in your dream, after this ghostly monk asked you where you hid it, you shouted at him that you'd never tell him?"

"Yes! I really thought I'd yelled out loud, it was so real."

Freya's thoughts were racing. "So, by saying you weren't going to tell him, ever, that indicates that you do know what he was after. Or you'd have shouted — hid what?"

Megan stared at her, realisation dawning. "Well, yes, I suppose so."

Jamie interrupted them. "Do you want to know what I think?"

Freya spun round, startled to find him right behind them. "Will you stop doing that? You scared us to death!"

"Come on girls, y'know you're dying to hear my slant on

the situ," Jamie went on, his gaze locked onto Megan.

"Actually, we're not," Freya retorted, linking her arm through her friend's. "And don't you know it's rude to eavesdrop on other people's conversations?"

Jamie loped alongside of them. "Well, when I overhear conversations that suggest someone's been reincarnated, I can't help but offer an opinion."

"Reincarnated!" Megan cried. "Who said I'd been reincarnated?"

"Ignore him," Freya warned. "Just because he reckons he's lived about three different lifetimes."

"Four — I've been getting flashbacks to my life during the Second World War. I mentioned that to you, didn't I, Megan?"

"Yes, and I'm still amazed you're taking it all so calmly. If you'd really got memories from a previous life you'd be as freaked out as…"

"As you?" he said looking sympathetically at Megan.

Freya's eyes fluttered shut. It wasn't a good idea to tell Jamie too much. But she could see by Megan's face that he'd got her hooked, even though she didn't answer.

"I was freaked out," Jamie told them, striding alongside of them. "It scared the life out of me to begin with. Then once I started to accept these flashbacks I found it fascinating. I write everything down now and try to work out who I was and when exactly I lived."

Megan stopped suddenly, dragging Freya to a standstill too. She looked up helplessly at Jamie, her eyes sad and pleading. "So what do I do?"

Freya groaned as she saw Jamie revel in the situation. "Well I find the best time to regress is just as you're drifting off to sleep. That's when I get my best memories. One of these days I'm going to a hypnotist to get regressed properly. That would be fantastic."

"Don't take any notice of him," Freya dismissed once

they were on their own again. "He's such a story-teller. The way he goes on about knowing me in a past life. If it was true, why can't I remember anything?"

Megan drew up her shoulders. "I don't know. Maybe we aren't supposed to remember. Maybe things just happen which reminds us, and then ghosts from the past creep up on you and try to make you remember... Freya, I'm really dreading going to sleep tonight. What if he comes back?"

Freya felt so sorry for her. "Tell you what, why don't we have a sleep over one night? Maybe your room won't be so spooky if there are two of us there."

"Tonight?"

"I can't tonight, it's my dad's birthday and we've got a family meal out. Sorry. Tomorrow though?"

"Okay, great. I'll sleep with the light on tonight," said Megan putting on a brave face.

"We'll get some DVDs and popcorn," Freya promised, pretending not to notice the stress behind her friend's eyes. She truly wished she could do something to help. But she didn't even know whether Megan had lived some previous existence, or whether her friend was just falling apart.

Chapter Thirteen
Talitha's Promise

1054 A.D. St. Mary's Priory, Coventry

Talitha was proud to be the handmaid of Prioress Godgifu. She had held the position for two years now, ever since she was fourteen. Talitha looked upon the gently pious Godgifu as almost saintly.

Godgifu was middle-aged now but in Talitha's eyes she was beautiful — and kind. She had taught Talitha how to read and write and how to pray. She showed her how to embroider and told her stories.

Talitha's favourite was of how Godgifu had argued one day with Leofric. He had wanted to increase the Heregeld taxes on the local people, and she had begged him not to.

He had thrown down the gauntlet. Mount your horse naked and ride through the market place and I will grant what you desire, he had said.

Chuckling, Godgifu had told Talitha that her husband never dreamed she would take him at his word. But she had done just that.

"Oh Talitha, dear child, you should have seen his face as I prepared for that ride. Everyone had been told to stay indoors. No one was to look, but I daresay one or two peeped out."

Talitha listened, never growing weary of the tale as she brushed Godgifu's long greying hair. "Yes, my lady, I imagine some roguish fellows would indeed have peeped."

Godgifu smiled at Talitha's reflection in the mirror. "My hair covered my modesty. It was longer and thicker in those days..." Her voice trailed away as if remembering something, and then rose suddenly. "Talitha, I have a request of you. You may say no, I would understand."

"I would never say no to you, my lady."

Godgifu looked into her eyes, and then taking her hand, led her along to the church. "There is whispering among the monks. They have heard rumours that a certain pendant in this church possesses magical powers. While I do not advocate magic and sorcery, I fear that it does exist."

Godgifu lowered her voice, as they entered the church. They walked slowly up the aisle, and only Godgifu's glance up at the statue of St. Osberga, indicated which pendant she was referring to. "The cross inlaid with gemstones?" she whispered. "Do you see the one?"

"Yes, my lady," Talitha answered, avoiding her eyes as Godgifu did, when two monks passed by.

When they had gone, Godgifu continued, "Each morning and each evening I look to see that it is still there, but I am growing old Talitha. I fear that after I die someone will take it, and should that person be of sin, and believe in selfishness and wickedness, then this world will suffer, because there will be no end to that evil."

"What do you ask of me, my lady?" asked Talitha.

"After I die, choose your time carefully when no one is around to see you. Take the pendant. It is called the Cross of Aes Dana — and it holds the power of immortality. Take it and find some place safe to hide it, where no one will ever find it. Promise me, Talitha."

"I promise," murmured the young handmaid.

And Talitha had kept her promise. A few days after Godgifu died, fourteen years later, Talitha had taken the Cross of Aes Dana and placed it where she could always keep check on it, to always be sure it was out of evil clutches. The safest place she could think of.

****

Megan slept with her lights on that night. She'd put some posters on the wall in an attempt to cover up the area where she'd seen the shadow. Yet even with the colourful images, she could still sense where the doorway had appeared. Eventually however, she fell asleep.

Talitha was there, in her dreams, waiting for her…

Her face, young and unblemished yet wreathed with sadness, hovered over Megan, mouthing incoherent words.

"I can't hear you," Megan murmured in her sleep. And again Talitha mouthed her silent plea. This time Megan heard the faintest of whispers, like a breath of wind.

She leaned closer, straining to catch the words. "Speak louder. I can't hear you."

And then, as clear as crystal, the words formed and echoed softly around Megan's head.

"Hide it Celeste. Hide it where no one will ever find it."

And with the words, Megan felt the small iron pendant in the shape of a cross, pressed firmly into her hands.

In her sleep she gripped the cross tightly and turned over into her pillow. "I will," she breathed softly. "I will."

****

Freya listened as Megan related her dream the next day at school. She was glad Megan had a better dream, and one which was shedding a bit of light on the mystery. "Well at least you know what your ghostly monk is on about now. And she called you Celeste? That's nice — it suits you."

"Thanks," Megan said, managing a small smile.

"So, this Talitha person who died when she was 184, yet only looked about... what?"

"Thirty," Megan reminded her.

Freya nodded. "Okay, thirty. And she's given you an iron cross pendant to hide where no one will ever find it. And this monk person is demanding to know where you've hidden it."

Megan heaved a sigh. "It looks like it."

"So maybe if you could remember where you hid it, you could tell him and he'd stop bothering you."

"No! I can never tell him!" Megan cried looking totally horrified at the prospect.

Freya stared at her. "Why? Why can't you tell him?"

"Because..." her voice trailed away as a look of helplessness drifted over her face. "I don't know. I... I've just got this awful feeling that if I tell him, then things will never be the same." She lowered her voice to a whisper. "I just feel that he's evil, and he must never know. He must never get his hands on it... I don't know why, it's just how I feel."

"But where did you hide it?" Freya asked softly.

Megan shook her head. "I've no idea."

After school they went back to Megan's house and had dinner with her parents. Mrs. Miller seemed less stressed and her dad was good fun, even though he embarrassed his daughter mercilessly, telling tales of the silly things she'd done over the years.

After dinner, followed by the most delicious cheesecake for dessert, Megan brought lots of photos up on her computer of old school friends and they chatted and laughed about normal things. Later still they made a huge box of popcorn and watched a couple of cheesy DVDs until they were both yawning madly.

By the time they got into bed, they both realised that they had barely given the shadow on the wall and ghostly monks a second thought.

"No more nightmares," Freya said, smiling as she snuggled down under the duvet.

"Absolutely not!" Megan agreed, turning off the light. "Goodnight!"

"Goodnight!"

It wasn't long before Freya could tell by Megan's breathing that she had fallen fast asleep. She was glad. She had looked so pale these last few days. A decent night's sleep would do her good.

Ten minutes or so later, just as she was drifting off, she realised that Megan was tossing restlessly in her sleep, as if she were dreaming. She was talking in her sleep too but the words were jumbled and made no sense. She hoped she wasn't locked inside another nightmare.

Freya spoke softly, hoping to banish any bad dreams. "You're dreaming Megan... Megan are you alright? Wake up Megan..."

Chapter Fourteen
Remembering Celeste

Megan's head had barely touched the pillow before she was asleep. Talitha was waiting for her, as if to remind her...

"Hide it Celeste. Hide it where no one will ever find it."

"Wait!" Desperately, Megan tried to open her eyes, to glimpse the pendant that Talitha had just pressed into her hand. She could feel the cool metal and the shape of a cross. There were stones encrusted into it. Her fingers traced them — six gemstones.

She desperately wanted to know their colour, but try as she might, her eyes refused to open so she could see. But then suddenly, without seeing them, she knew their colours: red, amber, and honey coloured stones. Hadn't she seen the pendant around Talitha's throat enough times to know their colours?

It was such a heavy pendant. Grey iron carved and ornately encrusted with gemstones. She had often wondered why her neighbour never took it off. Sometimes it seemed to weigh so heavily around her neck...

"Hide it Celeste. Hide it..."

"Why?" She called out in her sleep, desperately trying to reach out to the fading image of the woman. But her body felt paralysed, she couldn't even lift a finger, let alone reach out and catch her.

The vision of Talitha faded but Megan clutched the pendant until the metal dug deep into her palms.

She tried to turn on her bedside lamp. If she switched it on now, surely she would catch a glimpse of the object she was holding so tightly.

She reached out, moving easily now, and her arm felt something soft beside her — instantly recognising the long soft curls of her little sister lying next to her in their bed.

"You're dreaming Megan... Megan, are you alright? Wake up Megan..."

The mattress was lumpy, made of straw, and from the far side of the room, came the sound of a man snoring and the softer breathing of another sleeping person — her parents, sleeping soundly as they always did. Her father worked hard as a stonemason and her mother grew crops and kept chickens and pigs. And curled up next to her was little Ruth, fast asleep. Nothing ever woke her.

But something had awoken Celeste, and as the moonlight shone through the gaps in the window shutters, she saw that someone was creeping in through their door. She saw the shadow, moving swiftly and quietly towards her bed.

There were twenty or so small houses in their village, many of them built by her father. As a stonemason, his skills were regularly called on to build houses as the village continued to grow. They were just a mile or so from the bustling market town. Outside, chickens scratched about in the yards, there were sties for pigs and pens for the goats. Everyone knew each other and was welcome in each other's homes. But even so, it was odd that their neighbour, Talitha, had just crept silently through their door in the middle of the night.

Perhaps she was still upset, Celeste thought. Earlier that day, someone had died.

Talitha's wretched sobs had echoed all around the village. By evening her eyes were red from crying and her hair was matted from running her fingers through it in misery. Celeste and her little sister had watched from behind the pig sty, puzzled why Talitha was grieving so badly for the death of old Hannah.

Hannah was the oldest inhabitant of the village. It came as no surprise to anyone that she should die. Yet Talitha's grief was so dreadful, so pitiful, Celeste and little Ruth had secretly watched her drag helplessly at the ornate metal cross around her throat, as if by dislodging it, snapping the slender chain on which it hung, it would in some way ease her anguish. And now, Talitha, in the pale grey light of dawn, was tiptoeing across the rush mats in their house.

Seeing that Celeste was awake and staring at her, Talitha put her finger to her lips, pleading with Celeste not to alert the rest of the family to her presence.

Curious, Celeste sat upright in bed. She had known Talitha all her life, for as long as she could remember Talitha had been there, living amongst them, always looking so young and pretty.

Kneeling beside Celeste, the pendant glinted in the dawn light. Barely making a sound Talitha lifted it from her neck and pressed it into Celeste's hand.

The hard iron cross felt heavy and she felt the gemstones against her skin.

"Hide it Celeste," Talitha whispered. "Hide it where no one will ever find it."

"Your cross?" Celeste puzzled. "But you always wear this. I've never seen you without it. Why give it to me?"

"Celeste, it is not for you to wear," Talitha uttered, her voice cracking. "Never, never wear it. Promise me you will never wear it. You must hide it where no one will ever find it."

"But it must be so precious…"

"It's a curse!" the older woman said with such emotion that Celeste shrank back against the wall.

Talitha's eyes were racked with pain. "And I've been cursed by it for so long… but don't wear it, sweet Celeste. I wouldn't wish that upon you. But hide it away forever, so that no one can use it, especially those who seek power and would do evil — untold evil for ever more. Evil that no mortal soul will be able to stop."

"I don't understand…"

"This cross, Celeste, the Cross of Aes Dana," Talitha explained, speaking so softly that Celeste had to almost hold her breath to catch what was being said, "was given to Godgifu by an Earl who had suffered the heartbreak of seeing armies slain while he lived on. With this cross comes the power that whoever wears it has the gift of immortality."

Talitha's eyes fluttered shut but not before Celeste saw the utter misery locked within their depths.

"But what's wrong with living forever?" Celeste asked. "I think I should like that, never having to die."

Talitha breathed a sigh. "Dear child, how innocent you are. Let me explain, but I must speak quickly, I don't know how much time I have left."

"I don't think my family will wake yet, they sleep so soundly," Celeste whispered, hearing their steady breathing.

Again Talitha smiled. A kindly smile even though her eyes and her face seemed to be becoming more etched in sadness with every passing second. "Know this Celeste. For many years, this cross hung around the statue of St. Osberga in Godgifu's priory church. But people began to hear of its powers. Many believed it truly held the power of immortality. Many years ago Godgifu told me that she feared it would fall into evil hands. She asked me to take care of it." She smiled wistfully. "I was her handmaid — just a little older than you are now. Godgifu was so lovely, so pure and holy. I could not refuse her."

Celeste sat upright, working out numbers in her head. "But Godgifu died more than 150 years ago... that would make you over 180 years old!"

Talitha's eyes crinkled, she looked so tired suddenly. "One hundred and eighty-four to be precise."

Celeste gasped, and from across the room, her parents stirred, vaguely disturbed by the sound. "You can't be! You look younger than my mother!"

"That cross which I have burdened you with has the power to keep old age — and death — at bay," Talitha explained. "Celeste, dear child, do you know how many loved ones I have seen born, grow up, grow old, and die? Can you imagine what it's like to watch your children and your grandchildren, and their grandchildren come and go... can you imagine the pain and grief I have endured?"

Celeste imagined the misery, and her eyes filled with tears as the awfulness of that sunk in. Wishing she could ease Talitha's anguish, she held her hand, surprised to find that her skin felt leathery now. Moments before it had seemed soft... young. "You were crying so bitterly when old Hannah died today. Was she..."

"My great, great, great granddaughter!" Talitha said brokenly. "I watched her grow into a young woman, I saw her bring up her own family and become old. And I saw her die." Tears suddenly fell from her eyes. Eyes that were now clouded and dull, with wrinkles of age forming around them. "But enough is enough. I have done my duty to Godgifu. I can bear it no more. But Celeste you must not take this burden on your shoulders. But you must hide it. Hide it where no one will ever find it. I have heard rumours that someone is desperate to get their hands on it."

"Who?"

"One of the monks from the priory. Friar Lucius — you may know him. He is the tallest of them all and walks around with his head bent and his hands clasped in prayer. But when I have walked near him, I shudder."

"He doesn't know you have it, does he?"

Talitha gave a little shrug and then rubbed her shoulder as if it ached. "People have been talking. A few people here already know, and they pity me the burden I have been carrying all these generations. Other people sometimes mention that I never look any older. So I just smile and thank them — and they go about their business."

Celeste studied her as the dawn light crept through the window. Talitha didn't seem so young now, her skin looked like parchment and wrinkles were gathering all around her face.

She squeezed Celeste's hand as she got to her feet. But her movements were slow, as if everything was starting to ache.

"Hide it Celeste. Hide it so that no one will ever find it. I must go now, I'm very tired."

Clutching the pendant tightly, Celeste watched Talitha shuffle out of their house. She was stooped, and as she disappeared into the darkness, Celeste felt that a very old lady was leaving.

Celeste lay awake, unable to sleep. Talitha's words and her own thoughts ran wildly through her head. Could this cross really stop people from dying? And if Talitha was really so old, what would happen to her now that she had taken it off?

Her fingers traced the gemstones and carvings of the pendant as question after question spun through her mind.

Then, as daylight broke, Celeste had her answer.

The sound of a woman screaming startled the others awake. Her parents and her little sister leapt out of their beds and ran to the door. Quickly Celeste pushed the cross under her pillow and followed them.

Outside, chickens were clucking and running around

frantically with all the commotion. Other villagers had rushed out too and saw that it was Maud — old Hannah's daughter, who was making all the noise.

The middle-aged woman was screaming hysterically and pointing into Talitha's house, crying and stamping her feet as if she just couldn't bear what she'd seen. Celeste's father pushed his way through the small crowd that had gathered at her doorway. Everyone stood, silently waiting. Only Maud's occasional cries and moans broke the silence of the dawn.

A minute later, Celeste's father came out. His face was ashen.

"See!" Maud cried. "I'm not going mad am I?"

Her father shook his head. "Would someone fetch the priest? I think prayers need to be said."

"What's happened?" Celeste begged, as her father closed Talitha's door and walked back into his own kitchen. Celeste followed. "What's happened, father? Please tell us what's happened?"

He slumped down onto a stool, his head in his hands. His wife comforted him, not knowing herself what had distressed him so.

"What did you see?" she asked.

"Talitha is dead," he said quietly.

"Dead!" Celeste cried. "But I was only talking to her a…" her voice trailed away. Of course Talitha was dead. She was 184 years old. She had removed the pendant that was keeping her young and alive — so she had died.

"Why was Maud screaming so much?"

Her father raised his eyes. "You don't need to know, Celeste. Talitha is dead, that's all there is to it."

But that wasn't all there was to it. And by the time the priest had come from St. Michael's church and two monks from the priory, the gossip was all over the village. Talitha hadn't just died in the night. She had crumbled away to a skeleton.

****

Freya couldn't settle. She sat up in bed watching her friend twitching and mumbling in her sleep.

She tried to catch what she was saying, but it was all too jumbled. And then Megan fell silent, but as Freya looked down on her sleeping face she saw that tears were trickling from her closed eyes.

****

Celeste and her little sister sat huddled together by the well, watching as some of the men carried Talitha's body from her house. Celeste had seen other burials, but this wasn't a normal body that was heavy and took four people to carry it in a box. They brought Talitha out in a sack. They carried it carefully, but it was obvious that one man could have slung it over his shoulder. There was so little left of poor Talitha.

They buried her quickly, out in the meadow, not even where the others were buried. It was as if they were frightened, as if she'd had some sort of curse on her, and that she'd contaminate all the other souls if they buried her close to the others.

Celeste watched, tears rolling down her cheeks.

"Don't cry, Celeste," murmured her little sister, putting her arms around her trembling shoulders. "She's gone to Jesus now. He'll look after her."

"I know," Celeste murmured. But at that moment, it didn't help.

"Shall we pick some flowers for her grave?"

Celeste wiped her sleeve across her eyes and blew her nose on her apron. "Yes, she'd like that."

They found poppies, buttercups, and forget-me-nots. So many that both their skirts were full of a colourful profusion of little flowers as they held the hems to make baskets.

CELESTE

"Do you think we've got 184 flowers yet?" asked Celeste as they carried them out towards the small mound of earth in the meadow where a small wooden cross was sticking up from the fresh earth.

"Why?" Ruth asked, breathing in the scent of the flowers.

"We have to put 184 flowers on her grave — one for every year of her life."

"She wasn't that old!" Ruth exclaimed, sitting down on the grass with her blue frock flared out, so she could start counting.

Celeste didn't argue. "We need a pot of water. Go and ask mother will you? I'll count. I don't want to make a mistake."

Ruth shook her fair curls in that way of hers, the blue ribbon father had bought from a trader did little to keep her hair under control as she skipped off towards their house. People were still milling about, not really getting on with their work. Still shocked at finding Talitha had crumbled away like that.

Perhaps the people who knew about the cross never really believed its powers, but they certainly would now.

The priest was busy, talking to people, but as Celeste gathered a final four flowers to make 184, she looked up to see a tall, dark figure approaching.

Instantly her blood ran cold. A monk, a tall monk, walking with his head bowed and his hands clasped in prayer. Walking directly towards her as she sat by Talitha's grave — Friar Lucius.

****

Freya lay still with just the bedside lamp casting its pale pink glow around the room. Megan had been talking in her sleep for hours. Desperately Freya tried to make out what she was saying but the words were streaming out at a frantic pace.

Her closed eyes were fluttering crazily and her limbs jerked spasmodically. But at least she'd stopped crying.

As Freya watched, she began to think that maybe her friend's problems were more serious than she thought. These dreams and memories were unnatural.

She had given up trying to wake her. She'd once been told that if you wake someone suddenly when they were sleepwalking, it could send them into shock — or worse.

And although Megan wasn't sleepwalking exactly, she was as good as — her mind was far, far away.

Suddenly Megan gasped and sat bolt upright in bed. Her eyes were wide and staring.

Freya jumped. "Oh! You scared me! Are you alright?"

Megan looked at her, although Freya felt as if she were looking straight through her.

"I thought you'd gone," she uttered.

"No, of course not. Where would I go this time of night?" Freya answered.

"For the water."

Freya swung her legs out of bed. "Oh, you want a drink? Hang on I'll get you some water. I can use this glass it's only had cola in it."

"Yes," Megan murmured, still staring blindly at the wall in front of her. "Hurry though, please hurry."

"Well, okay, I'll be as quick as I can," Freya answered, taking the glass through to the bathroom.

By the time she returned, Megan was lying on her side, fast asleep — and talking to someone in her other world again.

Freya could have cried.

She hoped and prayed that her friend wasn't sick in the head, but on the other hand if Megan really had lived before, wasn't that even more mind blowing?

A stupid idea crossed her mind about texting Jamie. He reckoned he knew all about reincarnation. Maybe it would help to speak to him. Although at two in the morning it probably wasn't the best time to contact him. Tomorrow — even though it was against her better judgment. Tomorrow she would speak to Jamie and see if he had any suggestions that might help.

****

Celeste could smell the sweet fragrance of meadow flowers and decided to count them again, keeping her head down, hoping that if she looked busy enough he would pass her by. But he kept right on coming, until his ominous form blocked out the sun and cast a cold, black shadow across the grave — and across Celeste.

For long moments she concentrated on her counting, forty-eight, forty-nine, fifty... but he stood there, watching her, and she could feel his eyes burning through her skull.

She had to look up. And when she did, she understood why Talitha disliked him so. He looked harsh and mean. His mouth was thin-lipped like a blood-red slash across his white face, his nose was long and pointed, like a crow, and his eyes glittered with pure evil.

"You've picked flowers for the woman who died?" he said. His voice was thick and heavy. She didn't like his voice.

She swallowed hard. "Yes. My sister has gone for a pot to put them in."

"How many have you picked?"

"I don't know," Celeste lied.

"Shall I help you count them?"

"No!" She jumped to her feet, scattering them across the mound of earth, looking for sight of Ruth coming back. "It doesn't matter how many. I... I just want to put them in a pot before they di—"

"Die," he finished the word for her. "Like poor Talitha. What a terrible shock. This is a small community. You must have known her well. How old was she?"

Celeste's eyes fluttered shut. This was the monk. The one Talitha had warned her about, and here she was, keeper of the pendant for a mere few hours and already almost giving the game away.

"I don't know how old she was, about thirty perhaps."

"Some say," he breathed, lowering his voice. Lowering his long hooked neck so that his beaky face looked like it might peck her at any second. "Some say she had a magical pendant that kept her young. Some say she was very, very old."

Celeste felt her colour rising, it scorched up her throat and into her cheeks so that they burned so brightly it made her eyes sting. "That's silly."

"Did you ever see her wearing a magical pendant?"

"No! And I don't believe in magic anyway."

"Don't you?" he asked drawing backwards, looking down on her now from beneath his black cowl. "But you look such a bright, intelligent little girl. You shouldn't close your mind to things just because you don't understand them."

She shrugged, wishing her face would cool down, and wishing Ruth would hurry up and come back.

"I have spoken to some of your good neighbours. They say she always wore an iron cross with jewels set in it. Some people say she was never without it — ever. Yet there was no sign of it on her body."

As the words hung in the air, Celeste felt compelled to answer. "She… she must have taken it off."

"Your father was one of the first to go into her house when the cry went up, isn't that right, little girl… what is your name? It's so unfriendly to not call you by your name. I am Lucius — Friar Lucius."

I know who you are! Celeste thought. *And I know you oughtn't be wearing the robes of the church.* "If you're accusing my father of taking something that wasn't his — he wouldn't!" she said grinding her teeth together as she met his black stare with equal hostility.

He half smiled. "I wasn't accusing him of anything, dear child... your name? What is your name?"

"Celeste," she answered begrudgingly.

"Celeste," he repeated, as if carving the word onto his soul. "My dear Celeste, you are all good people. If anyone has that cross now, I think it would have been given to them by Talitha, God rest her soul, as a gift, or for safe keeping."

"Maybe it rotted away!" Celeste retaliated, her heart thudding as she stood up to this man who was twice her height and build. "I know what they found. She wasn't like a normal dead body, just looking like she was asleep. She'd rotted away. She'd turned into a skeleton. Well probably her jewels rotted away with her."

He looked at her for long, steady moments, his dark eyes glittering, considering her suggestion. "I said you were an intelligent little girl, didn't I, Celeste? Perhaps that is exactly what did happen."

From the corner of her eye, she spotted Ruth strolling back this way, carrying a jar carefully, so that she didn't spill the water. Celeste longed to shout at her to hurry up, but she had to stay calm and not let this monk know how afraid she was.

He sensed her distraction and glanced back over his shoulder. "Ah! Your sister has a vase. I think it's very kind of you to place flowers on Talitha's grave. The other villagers seem quite afraid to come and pay their respects. No one else has given her flowers, yet she was well liked, wasn't she?"

"Yes," Celeste answered, then called out to her sister. "Hurry up Ruth, the flowers are wilting."

"I'm coming."

"But you are not afraid," he said in a whisper, a whisper that sent shivers down her spine. "They are afraid because they don't understand. You however aren't afraid — is that because you do understand? You don't think her death and demise is because of sorcery or magic. I would almost think that Talitha, God rest her soul, had explained things to you. Told you of the jewelled cross she had taken charge of for so long. Perhaps she had explained that it kept her young, kept her from growing old and dying? Did she? Did she, Celeste?"

"No!"

Ignoring her denial, he went on, towering over her, trying to suck the truth from her. "Did she tell you that she was removing the cross? Did she tell you that she would die, once she removed it? That the years would catch up with her. How many years, Celeste?"

His eyes swivelled and he stared down at the flowers on the mound of earth. "How many years? How many flowers? Let's count them, shall we?"

Celeste backed away, colliding with her little sister.

"Mother says we are to be careful with the pot and not break it..." Ruth stopped as she saw the flowers scattered all over the mound. "Oh no! All our pretty flowers!"

"Let me help you," the monk said to Ruth, getting down on his knees to gather them in his large bony hands.

"It doesn't matter, we can do it!" Celeste stated, wanting him to go, to leave them alone. But he was on his knees, kneeling on the soft mound of earth that covered what was left of Talitha's body.

He ignored her, placing some of the flowers into the vase, smiling at Ruth. "You have picked a lot. There must be two hundred meadow flowers here."

Celeste knew what was coming, she heard Ruth's reply even before her little sister had opened her mouth. But there was nothing she could do to stop her.

"One hundred and eighty-four," said Ruth proudly, as if she was pleased to have remembered such a big number. "One for..."

"Every inch of the pot," interrupted Celeste, flashing her sister a look which she hoped would silence her. "We have to go now. My mother has chores for us to do. Come along Ruth."

"But we have to finish the flowers," Ruth argued, placing some flowers into the vase. "It was your idea anyway."

Knowing it would look strange to run now, Celeste gathered as many flowers as she could and squeezed them into the jar. "There! All done," she announced, placing it at one end of the mound. She would have liked to have stayed and said some prayers. She would do so later. For now, she just wanted to get away from this monk and his questions. She gave her sister a little push. "We have to go."

They'd walked a dozen steps when Friar Lucius called out her name. With a sinking heart, Celeste turned and looked back. He had risen from his knees, although two imprints had moulded themselves into the soft mound of earth.

"Yes?" she asked hesitantly.

He curved a long bony index finger, indicating she came closer.

Swallowing hard, Celeste took a step in his direction, while at the same time he took two long strides so that he was towering over her once more.

Closer than ever now, so close that she could smell his rancid hot breath on her face, making her want to turn away.

"Celeste," the word came out on a breath. "Where have you hidden it?"

She had no words. She wanted to sound aggrieved, to deny it, to be angry that he could accuse her of having it. But the words stuck in her throat and her face scorched, condemning her as fiercely as if she'd admitted clutching the pendant in her hand only a few hours before when Talitha had begged her to hide it. She did the only thing she could. Turning away from him, she ran.

"Wake up Megan! Megan, please wake up, you're dreaming... Megan! You're worrying me..."

"You're not to talk to him," Celeste uttered as she and

Ruth raced back to their house. "He's a bad man."

"But he's a monk," Ruth argued, her fair eyebrows crinkling as she scowled petulantly. "Monks work for our Lord Jesus Christ, so he must be good."

"I fear he is far from good, Ruth. Now hurry please," she said, holding her sister's hand tightly to make sure she didn't lag behind. Her thoughts were racing — imagining someone bad like him living forever, never dying. He could do all sorts of wicked things and there would be nothing anyone could do about it. His evil ways would live forever. No wonder Talitha had begged her to hide the pendant so people like him couldn't get their hands on it.

But where to hide it? Where?

Someone was shaking her. She looked around, trying to see who it was. Someone was talking to her — it sounded a bit like Ruth, only Ruth was hurrying along beside her, holding her hand, as silent as a mouse for once.

"Wake up... Please, wake up, you've been tossing and turning and mumbling for ages. Wake up please..."

"I'm not asleep," Celeste answered, turning to look at the person who had spoken.

She stared at the girl with the short sleek blonde hair. She looked so like her little sister it was uncanny.

Celeste wanted to ask her why she thought she was asleep but a wave of exhaustion washed over her suddenly and every scrap of energy drained from her body. Her eyes closed. "Oh I'm so tired. So very tired..."

Chapter Fifteen
Time Has No Barriers

"Your mum's brought us tea and toast," Freya said, opening the curtains and glancing uncertainly at her friend. She'd been half tempted to tell Mrs. Miller about the bad night her daughter had just had, then decided against it. It might just have been normal dreams brought on by too much junk food before bed.

Megan yawned and stretched. "Great, I'm starving. Although I don't know why after all that popcorn we ate last night. Sleep okay?"

"No, not exactly."

"Oh, why?" Megan asked, munching on a piece of toast.

Freya could almost have laughed. "Well because you were tossing and turning and talking in your sleep all night. You were having a right old garbled conversation with someone all night long."

"Oh, sorry. You should have woke me and told me to shut up or turn over."

Freya groaned. "Don't think I didn't try. But you were completely zonked out. Actually I was worried in case you were having another nightmare."

Megan shrugged and devoured the last bite of toast before grabbing another piece. "No, I don't think so. I don't feel freaked out or anything."

"So what were you dreaming about?" Freya asked curiously.

Megan thought for a moment. "I've no idea. Anyway, come on, we've got to get ready for school… but I am sorry if I kept you awake. You can blame me if you fall asleep in Mr. Kelly's maths lesson."

They walked to school, chatting about the DVDs they'd watched last night, and Freya was relieved to see that her friend wasn't stressed out about stuff today. Even so, she was definitely going to have a word with Jamie. Perhaps he could suggest a way of figuring out whether Megan had lived before — or if it was all in her head.

Reaching the school main doors, Freya spotted Jamie just coming through the school gates. Swiftly she made up an excuse to nip off and speak to him leaving Megan to go into class without her.

Feeling quite guilty at going behind her friend's back, Freya hurried over to the gates, anxious to catch Jamie while he was alone.

****

Megan couldn't help wondering what was so urgent that Freya had to speak to Jamie before class. Everyone was streaming into school, a whole brigade of royal blue, grey, and white. Lots of the kids said hello to her now, and she knew quite a few outside of her own class by name.

She stood there, vaguely aware that everyone was having to walk around her to get through the doors, but her gaze was fixed on Freya and Jamie.

As usual he was wearing his dark hooded top. He looked

so tall next to Freya that he had to stoop to catch what she was saying. Megan watched him standing there listening to Freya, his hands clasped together in front of him... as if in prayer.

Megan stared. He reminded her of someone...

Her blood ran cold.

Lucius!

His hooded top seemed to extend suddenly to his ankles. He looked up from beneath the cowl — looked directly at her with those cold hard eyes, and stormed straight towards her.

Megan's head swam. There were flowers all around her — poppies, forget-me-nots, buttercups. How many? Keep your eyes down, he might go away... don't look...

Then a dark shadow fell over her and a voice said, "You've picked flowers for the woman who died?"

A kaleidoscope of images flashed before her eyes — picking flowers, poor Talitha being carried out of her house in a sack, old Maud weeping and wailing, Talitha placing a gemstoned cross in her hand. The images ran through Megan's head like someone rewinding a film.

She stood, oblivious to people going into class, blind to the peculiar glances cast her way. She stood rigid, not uttering a word out loud, but in her head she was screaming. *"Ruth come here! Come here now!"*

Her little sister turned and smiled, then said something to the monk before skipping over to her.

"What was he saying to you?" Celeste demanded.

"He was just asking my name."

Celeste spoke seriously to her little sister. "You're not to talk to him. Do you understand?"

"But that wasn't..."

"But nothing! You're not to talk to him," Celeste told her sternly.

"Celeste..."

A harsh dark voice nearby startled her. She felt his unpleasant aura even before she turned and saw Friar Lucius.

The shadow he cast was as black as his heart and Celeste instantly shrank back.

The white crow-like face craned down on her and she could smell the dank rancid stench of evil.

"Do you know it's a sin to tell lies?"

She felt her cheeks glow pink. "I haven't told lies."

"But that's another lie... because you have lied to me. I asked you where you've hidden the cross Talitha wore, and you say you know nothing about it. But that is a lie. We both know it's a lie."

Her face was on fire and her eyes darted this way and that, wishing someone would save her. But no one objected to a man of the church talking to her. Even if he was hovering over her like a hawk about to tear into the flesh of a mouse it had cornered.

His breath was unpleasantly warm on her face, making her turn away. From the corner of her eye she glimpsed the tall steeple of St. Michael's church. The afternoon sunlight was glinting off the weathercock and the contrast of the goodliness of Jesus' house and the evil of this man overshadowing her made her dizzy.

"Lying is a sin. And sinners burn in hell. Do you want to burn in hell, Celeste?"

"No," she uttered.

"So I will ask you one more time, and if you tell me the truth, your sins shall be forgiven. Now where did you hide it?"

"Megan!"

A voice drifted through her thoughts, calling out to someone named Megan. Her hand went to her throat, startled. The voice seemed more in her head than in reality. Her fingers clutched the posy of herbs around her neck. At the same second the monk's demonic eyes followed the movement and stared at the cloth pouch she wore, as if it were a prize.

"Celeste! Ruth! Come in now, your mother has put your

meal on the table. We are all waiting."

Her father's voice now, but Celeste was locked in the cold, hard stare of the monk. She instinctively knew what he was thinking — that the pendant was in the pouch around her neck.

"Celeste! Hurry now!" her father called again.

Friar Lucius reached out, as if to grab the pouch but Celeste backed off. "You know where it is," he hissed. "Either it is around your own throat, or buried with the old woman's bones."

Celeste didn't wait another second. She ducked under his arm and raced into her house, slamming the door behind her.

"Thanks!"

"Megan! You slammed the door right in Jamie's face! Megan... Are you okay? Speak to me will you?"

"Hello! Earth calling Megan, anyone home?"

Someone was shaking her arm. She turned and saw the face looking down at her from behind a dark hood.

"Leave me alone!" she screamed, twisting free and backing away.

"What's up with her?"

"Megan, it's okay... It's us... Oh Jamie! She looks terrified!"

"Hey, chill," said Jamie, his hands reaching out from under his dark robe's sleeves, trying to grab her again. "Man! Look at her eyes! She's totally freaked out."

"Oh Jamie, what can we do?"

Megan stared at the two anxious faces staring at her. Others were weaving around her. Everyone was dressed similarly — in uniform — school uniform. She was in school — not at home in her village about to have dinner with her family. She was in school, even though she could smell the thick broth her mother had made... she was in school, and her parents would be long dead by now.

Her knees buckled.

"Catch her Jamie!"

"I'm... I'm alright!" Megan uttered, fighting back the swampy blackness that almost engulfed her and frantically wriggling free from Jamie's grip.

Freya looked anxiously at her. "Megan, what brought that on? Was it Talitha again?"

"She's dead," Megan murmured shakily, desperately trying not to let herself think about her parents.

"What happened?"

"She took the cross off, and she died," she spoke flatly, feeling as if every scrap of emotion had been drained from her body. "It's called the cross of Aes Dana and it has the power to grant the wearer everlasting life. Talitha wore it for a hundred and fifty years. She took it off and crumbled away to a skeleton."

Freya clasped her hand over her mouth.

Jamie looked intrigued. "So when did all this happen? Can we work out any dates?"

"Probably, if you know when Lady Godiva died?" Megan answered dully.

"Well, I'm pretty sure she was around from the beginning of the 11th century to about 1067-ish," said Jamie, growing more animated by the second.

They headed towards class, and as they walked along the corridors Megan described the memories she'd just re-lived. But she spoke flatly, devoid of emotion. Freya listened in stunned silence while Jamie seemed entranced.

"This is just incredible," he exclaimed, loping along in that way of his, hands clasped in front of him, his hood half hiding his face.

Megan cast him a sideways glance. She felt odd. Her skin was prickling.

Deep inside, her heart was aching unbearably for the parents who were now lost to her. She felt as if her heart was breaking.

But despite that — despite that misery, her skin was prickling.

Jamie…

He believed he'd lived before. He thought he was a Benedictine monk from the Priory. The way he walked, hands clasped in prayer. The way he sneaked up behind you unexpectedly. The way he was questioning her now, sucking out all the information he could from her.

She felt light headed.

Surely not Jamie… Oh please, not Jamie!

Reaching class, everyone was seated and Mrs. Lovejoy was about to call the register. As they headed for their desks, Jamie caught her arm.

Lowering his head so that his mouth was close to her ear, he whispered softly, "So where did you hide it?"

Dumbstruck, Megan's blood ran cold.

Hundreds of years on, yet nothing had changed.

Jamie… Lucius, whoever he was, was still desperate to get his hands on the Cross of Aes Dana.

Chapter Sixteen
Hidden Away

Black coils of mist swirled around his ankles, and the stench of evil told him the demons were back. They never left him alone for long; they constantly taunted him, reminding him that his descent into hell was long overdue.

This time he welcomed them.

He clasped his hands tightly together, bowed his head to plead with them and all the other heinous devils that inhabited the depths of hell.

He called upon them all to hear his plea.

"Life is what I beg for. Grant unto me a short spell of life once more. Release me from this spirit world and reunite me with my healed mortal body. And when that short period of life is extinguished I shall offer no resistance. I shall face my destiny. My soul shall be yours."

He heard the demonic shrieks of laughter as they mocked his request. But he persisted, knowing even they could not see the deepest darkest part of his black soul — the part that intended to trick these demons and devils.

His plan was simple. Once he was granted this one small

request, once he was a mortal again, then he would find the Cross of Aes Dana. And when it was his, his life would be extended forever. Demons and devils could go to hell and stay there.

How could they take his soul, when it would be again attached to his living, breathing flesh and blood body? A body that could never die.

Dropping to his knees he continued to plead with them.

****

Megan hadn't felt much like talking for the rest of the day and she deliberately avoided Jamie even though half of her — the normal half, craved his company. After school she and Freya walked back home to pick up Freya's overnight bag.

"How are you feeling?" Freya asked as they took a shortcut across the green towards Megan's house.

"Weird," Megan answered. "I'll be glad to see my mum and dad tonight actually. At least this set of parents is still around."

Freya smiled sympathetically. "Do you think they're the same? I mean, your parents now — were they your parents then?"

Megan shrugged. She'd been asking herself that same question all day. "I've no idea. I don't know how this reincarnation thing works."

"I just wish Jamie knew more about it. He's always going on about it."

"There's something else," Megan interrupted her.

"Oh?"

She took a deep breath. "That monk... Friar Lucius..."

"What about him?"

Megan glanced around, half expecting Jamie to leap out on her. "I'm so afraid that Jamie and Lucius are the same person."

Freya burst out laughing. But then her laughter died. "No! Not Jamie. He's nice! Well, in a weird kind of way. That Friar Lucius you've been telling us about is absolutely horrible. What on earth makes you link them together?"

Megan kept her eyes peeled for Jamie. At the speed he walked he'd be home by now and while she wasn't sure exactly where he lived, she guessed it was close or he wouldn't walk his dog around here.

"It's just a feeling," she tried to explain. "It's partly because of how he walks with his hands clasped in front of him, that's how Lucius walked. And because he remembers being a monk, and because…" She took another deep breath. It was the moment to tell Freya that they were sisters. But then she spotted Jamie far off in the distance walking Sally and the moment passed. Her heartbeat quickened. "There he is. Don't tell him if he comes over. Please don't tell him."

"Okay! Don't worry, I won't."

Megan walked faster, anxious to get home before Jamie spotted them. "You know Freya I can still hear my dad calling u… me in for dinner. We were having chicken broth. I can still smell it. It's thick with barley. I can see us all sitting at the table. I'm mopping up the gravy with a chunk of bread." Her voice rose. "Someone's crying!"

"I can't hear anybody," Freya said, glancing around. Then she looked back at Megan. "Oh! You mean back then… who? Who's crying?"

Megan stood quite still, listening to someone wailing. It was coming from outside their door. Her father opened it, and they saw Maud slumped in the doorway, head in hands, wailing and pointing off into the distance — to where they had buried Talitha that morning.

"It's Maud, one of Talitha's descendants," Megan explained, seeing both worlds quite clearly as if she were looking at life through a split screen. "I can hear what she's saying… She says he's digging up Talitha's grave. Bad enough they bury her in unhallowed ground, but now he's defacing that too."

"You can see all that?" Freya breathed, gaping at her friend as they stood statue-like in the middle of the field.

"My father looks so angry and my mother is trying to comfort her. Wait! Listen... Maud's speaking again... she says it's Friar Lucius. Maud went to the grave to say prayers and found him there, on his knees, digging up the grave with his bare hands, like a mad man."

Megan looked wildly at Freya. It was strange, her friend seemed to be fading, as if a veil was covering her, while her ancient world was becoming clear as day. "I know what he's up to. He's looking to see if they buried the cross with Talitha. I have to hide it, quickly, but where?"

"Megan, stop now, that's enough!" Freya ordered, her voice rising in panic. "You're slipping back in time again. Come back to me. Please don't go back, please don't..."

Celeste looked frantically around, and in the distance saw the spire of St. Michael's Church. "I know where I can hide it. I'll have to be quick. I need to gather some things together — father's mallet and chisel. Find me a sack to wrap them in. Hurry!"

"Megan! Stop! Stop this! Megan come back... Please!"

With the cross and her father's tools wrapped in the sack, Celeste secretively slipped away from the house. Once clear of the village, she ran. For a time she heard that voice in her head again, the one that sounded like Ruth, but it was calling to someone called Megan. Celeste didn't have time to try and work it all out. She kept right on running until the voice pleading for Megan to come back faded away until finally she couldn't hear it at all.

She didn't stop, even though her parcel weighed heavily in her arms, she ran on until she reached the milestone that said Couaentree was just a half mile away.

Celeste knew the route well but she glanced back

constantly, fearing she would see him striding after her. Like a stalking monstrous black crow lurching after its prey, ready to pounce and kill.

Thankfully, the pathway through the woods remained deserted. She raced on, clutching the package that weighed heavier with every step until she reached the town. Cobbled streets opened up before her and the countryside fragrances of lavender and wild garlic were masked by less pleasant smells.

Celeste walked quickly through the crowded narrow streets to where the church of Saint Michael stood waiting.

The cool of the building was a welcome relief and she blessed herself with holy water from the little dish inset in the wall and genuflected before the beautiful crucifix with Jesus nailed to it.

Gripping the package fiercely despite its weight, she walked towards the back of the church, her soft shoes making scuffing sounds on the cold floor. Some of the large stone slabs she walked over had names and dates carved into them. And the sunlight sparkling in through the stained glass windows made prisms of colour dance before her eyes.

She reached the narrow arched doorway that led up to the spire and her heart began to race faster. Were ordinary people like her allowed up into the spire? She had no idea. Holding her breath, she stepped through the doorway and came face to face with a monk emerging from the shadows.

Celeste stumbled to a halt, so stricken with panic she felt her heart jump into her mouth.

"Forgive me," he murmured, moving aside so she could pass.

She glimpsed his face. It was a pleasant, young face — not *his* face. She recognised him as the young monk who accompanied Lucius into their village on the morning of Talitha's death. Turning her face quickly away in case he recognised her, she waited until he had gone before starting up the spiral staircase. It was long moments before her racing heart beat normally again.

With a glance back, she began her climb, there was no time to lose. She counted as she went, her feet scuffing against each stone step, her free hand following the sweep of the sandstone wall. The brickwork felt cold and damp against her skin as, breathlessly, she climbed on, going higher than she had ever been in her life.

At the one hundred and eighty-fourth step she stopped and caught her breath. There were small slats in the outer wall, enabling her to peer through. She looked down onto the church roof, and the priory, and the treetops, and distant houses with wisps of pale grey smoke drifting up from their chimneys.

She climbed on, her feet in buttoned-up shoes tripping up the stone steps, one after another, after another. Her fear growing that he would come after her. That somehow he would know where she had gone.

After what seemed an eternity of climbing, a shaft of daylight brightened the stairs ahead and the chill of the air told her that she was almost at the top. A few more steps and an open doorway led her out onto the turreted balcony.

A cold wind blew across her face, fluttering her hair over her eyes as she ventured out into the open. She felt quite heady from being so high — higher than any tree she had climbed, almost as high as the clouds.

Cautiously, she walked to the turreted wall and peeped over, catching her breath at the spectacular view. She could see St. Mary's Priory in its entirety — how enormous it was, and she could see the rooftops of the town houses, beyond which lay a patchwork of greens, browns, and yellows. Cattle looked as small as mice and the rivers looked like silver ribbons.

Some people thought that the world was flat, and if you walked far enough you would fall off the edge. But Celeste had heard stories from the elders that a great explorer discovered the world was round like an apple. From here she could see that for herself. The horizon wasn't straight at all — there was the gentlest of curves. And if she let her imagination flow, she could almost imagine how big the world was.

But she had no time for daydreaming. She had to work quickly. If her parents realised she wasn't playing somewhere in the village, they would come looking for her and she could guess who would be leading the search.

Concentrating on her task, Celeste chose the spot — the far corner of the north-facing wall, where the sun would least shine — a shadowy, unspectacular corner of St. Michael's spire.

Opening the sacking parcel, she placed the pendant to one side and took up the mallet and chisel that she had carried all this way. Selecting a half brick, she began to chisel it loose from the wall, smothering the chisel end with sacking to deaden the sound as she chipped away.

She had watched her father work with stone. He had taught her how to wield a hammer, but still it took much longer than she had envisaged.

Determination forced her on, even though her arms and hands ached. Finally, the brick began to move. Waggling it, levering it, willing it to come loose, it eventually came away in her hand.

Celeste stared at the small secret cavity it revealed.

Heart thudding, looking back over her shoulder constantly, she placed the pendant as far into the cavity as it would go, then chipped away at the piece of brick that had to be replaced. At last, the sandstone brick slotted back smoothly and she wedged it into place with other remnants of the soft red stone. Finally, she stood back to inspect her work.

There was nothing to say the brick had ever been disturbed. She had done a good job. Gathering up the final chippings and sandstone dust, she released them over the turrets into the wind.

She watched the colourful specks blow away on the

breeze, and then with a final glance back at the wall, she turned and fled back down the three hundred steps and out into the evening's fading sunlight. She was tired and weary. Never had she known such a long and exhausting day. The birds were coming home to roost, their singing voices filled the treetops, and the sun was rapidly sinking into the distance. Now the sky was blood red, streaked with silver and the shadows were gathering.

She was almost home. The big oak tree where she often played was a welcome landmark. Soon she would turn the bend by the river and see the clutch of little houses. No doubt she would have some explaining to do. She had been gone so long.

Suddenly she sensed a rustle in the undergrowth, a movement amongst the bushes, her step faltered.

A tall, black figure rose up before her eyes.

Lucius stood in front of her, barring her way, his sharp eyes glinting with delight — like a fox with a hen it was about to rip to shreds.

His mouth moved into a snarl and from beneath the folds of his robe he produced a dagger. Thin and sharp with a handle of bone, its steel glinted in the dying rays of the sun.

The forest fell silent. It was as if all the birds were shrinking back, afraid of this monstrous evil man.

He took a step towards Celeste, the steely tip of the dagger pointed directly at her throat. His voice was a rasp, as he spoke. "I will ask you one last time, child, where did you hide it?"

Celeste screamed.

Chapter Seventeen
Flashbacks

As usual Sally bounded excitedly across the common following her usual zigzag trail. Jamie strode along behind, keeping an eye on his dog in case she went too deep into the thicket as she'd done before.

There were quite a few kids out playing now and people walking their dogs. In the distance he spotted Megan and Freya, they were just standing there — or rather Megan was. Freya was looking pretty agitated, like this morning at school when Megan had gone into a trance.

He stood and watched for a moment.

He wasn't prepared for the icy cold sensation that swamped him. But the moment he felt the chill he knew he was in for another vision from his past. The feel of a heavy, woollen dark robe shrouding his body and sandals on his feet told him where his mind was drifting.

He expected to see little Freya standing before him again, dragging at his sleeves, looking up at him with such desperation in her eyes.

But instead he saw a flash of steel — a dagger. A dagger

with a long thin blade. Its cream-coloured boned handle was ornate. And then as if a crimson veil had been thrown over him, his world was flooded red.

Cloying and sticky, blood dripped from his hands, drenched his robe. Dark red blood that could only come from the deepest of veins.

Seconds later the veil lifted. His world was green and brown again. Sally was prancing around his ankles. Kids were playing; people were walking their dogs.

Jamie dropped to his knees, head bowed. Thinking he was playing, Sally took the opportunity to lick his face.

Then, rising unsteadily to his feet, Jamie focused ahead, on Megan and Freya.

Purposefully he strode out towards them.

****

"Thank goodness you're here Jamie," Freya cried, glancing briefly at him as he reached her. "Look at the state she's in! She's gone back in time again, only it's worse than ever. She's been like this for ten minutes — I don't know what to do. I'm really frightened for her. What if she never comes out of it? I'd better get her mum, hadn't I? She's going to freak!"

"Let me see if I can reach her," Jamie said, standing directly in front of Megan and gripping her arms. "Megan! Come back now. You're needed here with your friends. Come back to us."

"Megan!" Freya joined in, squeezing her friend's hand. "It's us — Jamie and Freya. Can you hear us? Oh Jamie, I think we need to call an ambulance."

Megan's glazed eyes suddenly focused on Freya. She squinted as if nothing made any sense to her. And then her gaze switched to Jamie and her whole body jerked. "Stay away from me!" she shrieked.

Freya jumped at the sudden violent outburst from her friend. "It... it's okay, Megan. It's just us, me and Jamie, and look, here's Sally. You remember Sally, don't you?"

Megan stumbled backwards, her eyes wide with terror. "Keep away!" she cried frantically scrabbling around for something, totally confused.

"What?" Freya sobbed, distraught at seeing her friend like this. "What is it?"

"Where's it gone? I had it a second ago. It must have slipped out of my hands. "Father will be so displeased if I've lost his..." Her eyes focused on Jamie again, and her hands went up in defence. "Stay away from me!"

Freya couldn't bear it. "No one's going to hurt you, Megan. We're your friends. You slipped back in time but you have to come back. You belong here. Oh Jamie what are we going to do? Look at her eyes she's not seeing us at all. She's miles away, she's in another world."

Megan stopped her frantic searching and stared at her, almost as if she couldn't believe her eyes. "Freya?"

"Oh! Thank heavens!" Freya uttered, shooting a relived glance at Jamie.

Megan turned her attention to the dog, the horrible vague look in her eyes clearing. "Sally?" She scooped the little dog up in her arms.

"You gave me such a fright," breathed Freya, trembling from head to foot. "The last thing you said was that you were going to hide the cross. Then you just stopped talking and went into a trance with your arms and legs all twitching and your eyes flickering, like you were having a fit standing up. You've been like that for ages, I was so scared you'd never come back."

"I'm sorry, I couldn't help it," Megan murmured, clutching the dog like it was a lifeline.

"What happened... where were you?" Jamie wanted to know.

Megan said nothing but her eyes flinched as if she deliberately didn't want to speak to him.

Freya glanced from one to the other, trying to work out what was going on here, and then remembered what Megan had said about Jamie and Lucius being one and the same. "She's not up to talking Jamie. She needs to go home."

But Jamie had other ideas. "It would be better if you talked about it, rather than bottling it all up."

Megan tried to turn away. "Another time, Jamie. I want to go in. My mum will have my tea ready."

He stepped in front of her. "Megan! This is important. Stop running away, will you!"

Seeing her friend jerk sharply as Jamie barred their way, Freya put her arm protectively around Megan's shoulders. "Tomorrow Jamie, or Monday, when we're back in school. She really needs to get in now."

"She really needs to talk this through, or get help or do some research and get to the bottom of this," he argued. Then his expression softened. "Look, it's Saturday tomorrow. I'm going to the library archives to try and research these monk memories that are bugging me. I need to know what's going on."

"You need to know!" Megan burst out. "I'm the one having all these insane flashbacks or whatever they are."

"You're not the only one, actually," he said, looking steadily at her.

"What do you mean?"

"My memories of being a monk are becoming clearer."

"They are?" Megan breathed.

"I had another vision, or whatever you want to call it when I was walking Sally a few minutes ago. I need to research that time period. If our past lives are linked my calculations reckon we were around in the early thirteenth century."

"And what if you don't like what you find?" Megan

suggested.

Jamie lowered his eyes. "I'm not expecting to like it."

"Meaning?" Freya demanded, hoping against hope that he wasn't going to say anything that would freak Megan out more than she already was.

He wrinkled his nose. "Nothing! Forget it. You'd better get home, Megan."

"Yes, come on," urged Freya but Megan stood rigid.

"What are you expecting to find out?" Megan demanded, her eyes glittering.

"Nothing. Doesn't matter."

"Yes it does!" she cried. "It's something to do with that flashback you just had, isn't it? What did you see? You saw yourself as a monk didn't you?"

"Yes."

"And what were you doing?"

He chewed on his lip, his eyes downcast. "I couldn't tell. It's fragmented, just flashes, like splinters of broken glass. But it... was pretty unpleasant."

Freya moved swiftly, snatching Sally from Megan's arms and placing the dog back with Jamie. "Right! That's enough! You're not going to scare her with your stupid stories..."

"Fine!" he said, turning to go.

But Megan wrenched free and grabbed his arm, stopping him. "You tell me what you saw, Jamie Monkman. You tell me everything!"

"Just leave it!" Freya begged.

"I want to know!" Megan implored, turning back to Jamie. "Tell me!"

The colour seemed to have drained from his cheeks and his eyes winced as if in pain. He took a deep breath. "Okay, if you really want to know, I saw a dagger — it had a long thin, razor sharp blade... I just saw a flash of it... and then..."

"What?" Megan demanded, while Freya held her breath.

He looked steadily at each one of them in turn and then

murmured. "I saw blood. So much blood."

****

Freya was furious with Jamie. How could he be so stupid, so insensitive? Couldn't he see that Megan was traumatised enough? Did he have to terrify her even more?

She sat on the edge of Megan's bed trying to reassure her that Jamie's imaginings had nothing to do with her. But she knew she was wasting her breath.

She could see it in her friend's worried eyes as she paced back and forth across the room. Megan thought it was her own blood he'd seen.

"What else can it be?" Megan wailed, practically wringing her hands together. "Lucius knew I'd got the cross. He probably thought it was in the pouch I always wore around my neck. He came after me… he was waiting for me in the woods. He must have attacked me. And if Jamie can remember that — it means he was Lucius!"

"Megan, your imagination is running away with you," Freya exclaimed, throwing her hands up. "Oh that Jamie, I could slap him. But as for him being a reincarnation of Friar Lucius, I still think that's crazy. He's annoying certainly, but evil, no, not Jamie! Besides, if he was Lucius wouldn't he remember you from his past life? It's me he remembers."

"Oh he remembers me alright," Megan said harshly. "But he's not going to admit that is he? He's just waiting to find out where I hid the cross."

"But you don't remember anyway."

"I do actually."

"You do?"

Megan nodded. "I hid it. In the old cathedral spire. In the brickwork. I was running home when he jumped out of the bushes… That's when Jamie's bloodied flashback comes in!"

An icy chill ran down Freya's spine. "No! Stop this

Megan you've no proof of any of it. And anyway, if Jamie was Lucius and he remembers me, why don't you remember me too? See, it just doesn't make sen..." Her voice trailed away as she saw the look on Megan's face. "What?"

Megan dragged her fingers raggedly through her hair. "I've been too afraid to tell you."

"Tell me what?" Freya demanded, goose bumps breaking out all over her skin.

Megan walked to the window and stared out. When she spoke her voice was barely a whisper. "I wasn't an only child."

"I know that, you had a little sister called Ruth," Freya said, her heart pounding suddenly.

Slowly, Megan turned and looked straight at her. "Yes, Ruth was five years younger than me."

"O-kay, and what else do you remember about her?"

"Everything," Megan breathed, looking at her so strangely that Freya felt as if her hair was standing on end.

Freya swallowed hard. "Tell me about her."

Megan squeezed her eyes shut, as if trying to hold everything back. The look on her face should have warned Freya, but nothing could have prepared her for what her friend was about to say.

"My little sister was called Ruth in those days. But I know her by another name..."

Freya held her breath. "Go on..."

"In this life her name is Freya."

****

At least Freya hadn't run screaming for the door. She'd just sat there, on the edge of the bed and Megan had watched every drop of colour drain from her face.

She didn't ask questions. Didn't argue against it, didn't suggest alternative ideas, she just sat silently, almost like a statue, absorbing the fact that she too had lived before.

"But I don't remember a thing!" she finally blurted out.

"I don't think we're supposed to remember," said Megan, longing to put her arms around her little sister and comfort her — but she was afraid that Freya would reject her, call her insane, scream at her that she didn't believe a word. So she kept herself under tight control. "I think my remembering all this is a big mistake. Something triggered my subconscious and unlocked a door to my past life when really it should have stayed locked."

Freya nodded, her head lowered.

Megan spoke softly. "I knew you, the moment I set eyes on you in class. I thought, Oh! There you are! As if I hadn't seen you in ages. Didn't you recognise me at all?"

Freya shook her head. "No. I did think you had a lovely friendly smile, but not for a second did I think you were my long lost big sister. I'm sorry."

Megan somehow stopped her chin from crumpling. "Just as well. What if everyone has lived before and we all remembered everything? Just think how confusing that would be."

"Yes, and how sad."

Her eyes fluttered shut as she thought about her parents. "Yes, so very sad."

Freya fell silent for a moment, and then asked, "So I was with you, when you put flowers on Talitha's grave?"

"Yes, you went to fetch a vase to put them in. I had a flash memory of you carrying that vase that day in town just after I saw that ribbon seller."

"And did I come with you, when you hid the cross in the spire?"

"No. I was in a mad panic. While Lucius was digging up Talitha's grave, I ran into town with father's mallet and chisel."

"And you think Lucius went after you."

Megan nodded.

"And murdered you?"

"What other explanation can there be?"

"So that memory Jamie has of me, pleading with him... I wonder if I was trying to stop him going after you. Maybe I was begging him to leave you alone."

"It makes sense. You would have tried to protect me, Freya, but neither of us stood a chance against him. He was so determined to get his hands on the cross... and still is."

"Are we going to meet him tomorrow to do some research?" Freya asked cautiously. "We don't have to. Maybe if you close your mind to it, all these flashbacks will stop."

Megan smiled weakly. "If only!"

Freya got up to leave then; she looked tired. Megan followed her to the door, her heart heavy.

"I'm sorry," Megan murmured, as her friend — her little sister left.

Freya glanced back and tried to smile. "There's nothing to be sorry about. I'm glad you told me. See you tomorrow by Lady Godiva's statue at ten, yes?"

Megan nodded, not knowing why she felt so downhearted. "Yes, ten o'clock. See you."

"See you."

That night Megan couldn't sleep. She lay in the dark, wondering when the nightmares would start. Then it dawned on her that all her worst nightmares had caught up with her. Lucius wasn't just in her head, wasn't just haunting her. He was here, somehow lurking within the body of a boy in her class with a weird pattern shaved in his hair. Even that tallied. Monks had the top of their heads shaved, leaving just a circle of hair. Jamie's style was more elaborate, but both styles were the fashion for the time — and for a monk. Oh heavens! And his name was Jamie Monkman! Groaning, she buried her face in her pillow, weeping tears for a boy in her class who she had liked — really liked. But he wasn't a boy — he was pure evil.

A while later her mobile phone beeped, telling her she

had a message. She rolled over and reached for it. Pressing the button, the screen lit up.

FREYA MOBILE: Don't worry we'll sort it. Luv Freya yr little sis x

Megan stared at the message until her eyes flooded with tears again, but not tears of misery this time. She tapped out her reply: Yeah, we will. Luv yr big sis M x

Then turning onto her side, still clutching her mobile, her tears drying, she slept soundly.

Chapter Eighteen
Reincarnate

I beseech you, demons of the darkest hell. Grant unto me a brief spell of mortality. Surely you can spare me that after all this time. We have come to know each other so well. You await my descent into hell's fires with eagerness. Make me mortal again and I will be all yours in a human lifespan, forty, sixty, eighty years. But as a spirit existing between worlds I am beyond your reach until I descend. And I have held you at bay these eight hundred years. I can hold you at bay for another thousand.

He listened, waited, aware of the demonic skittering around his feet and above his head; he heard their screeches of laughter again as they mocked him. And then the largest of the demons slithered closer, its head inclined to one side.

He was ready to plead once more, and this time he sensed they would grant his wish.

Lucius would live again.

****

As the carved wooden Godiva hobbled around its track, Megan spotted Freya walking through the precinct towards her. She waved. To her delight, Freya broke into a run and practically dived on her.

"Hiya! How's my big sister this morning?"

Megan's heart swelled. "Good! Really good!"

"Feeling up to seeing Jamie?"

"Hope so... Oh there he is. Oh! My!" She stopped in her tracks. He looked different in white jeans and a bright blue T-shirt with a cartoon penguin on the front — and without his hooded jacket for once. He looked normal — and gorgeous. For a second, thoughts about him being a murdering monk vanished from her head.

"I texted him," Freya hissed. "Told him he shouldn't look like a hoody if we're to get anywhere with the archivist."

Megan discovered that she could still smile. "Good idea. I don't think the penguin is going to impress anyone though."

He spotted them, and as if on a whim took their photo on his mobile phone as they walked towards him. "Y'know what? You two could almost pass as sisters. How are you both today anyway?"

"We're good," Freya answered, casting Megan a secret glance. "Glad to see you've dressed for the occasion!"

Jamie grinned. "I know. The penguin is almost as cute as me."

Megan struggled not to laugh.

"Hey! A smile! I thought you'd run out of those."

She gave a little shrug, deep down wishing... wishing with all her heart that he were just a normal boy, and not a demonic, murdering monk hiding behind a mask of normality.

Jamie led the way through to the archives. It was similar to a library except the books were mainly behind glass. The archivist first gave them white cotton gloves to wear, to protect the ancient documents, then went off to find the books they needed.

Jamie had asked for documents and records from Godiva's priory and local maps of the area for the thirteenth century. The archivist came back with two massive old leather-bound books and even bigger charts showing the landscape of the time.

She raised her eyebrows as she settled the books onto a table. "Has our time-traveller roped you girls into helping him with his research?"

"Yes, something like that," Freya answered vaguely.

"The archivist knows me," Jamie remarked as the woman went in search of more volumes. "I'm something of a regular here. But at least now I'm pretty certain that I know what era I lived in when I was a Benedictine monk."

Megan studied him. He was very good at keeping up the pretence of innocence. But she wasn't about to drop her guard. Lucius was smart, she had no doubt he would try and trick her into giving away the truth about where she had hidden the cross.

"I was doing some calculating last night," Jamie continued. "And going by Talitha's age when she died and bearing in mind she was handmaid to Godiva, I reckon that you Megan, existed around the year 1221 — obviously before and after, but somewhere around that time."

Megan lowered her voice to a whisper so only Freya could see her lips form the words, "Not after, that's for sure."

"You don't know that," Freya whispered back.

Megan gave a sad little shrug.

Jamie rubbed his gloved hands together. "Well I'm going to make a start on this monster — The Chronicles of Warwickshire by Roger de Wendover. Oh, Megan, by the way, I don't suppose you've had any more flashbacks revealing where you hid the cross thing yet, have you?"

"No. It's all very vague," she lied, her cheeks colouring as swiftly as they did that day at Talitha's graveside, eight hundred years ago. She half expected him to remind her that lying is a sin.

"Oh well," he shrugged, as if he didn't really care one way or the other. He carefully opened the hefty book. "Right, do not disturb, genius at work."

The girls started by examining a map that showed Coventry, or Couaentree as it was spelled on the parchment sheet. The massive priory was sketched onto it, and scattered beyond the main town, little clusters of houses were dotted amongst the forests.

"It actually makes sense," Megan said, following a dotted line with her finger. "I've walked this path into town so many times. Our house was one of these," she said pointing. "And just about here, was an absolutely massive oak tree. You could stand on its branches and not worry about falling off."

Jamie glanced up. "How come you remember unimportant things like trees, when you can't remember where you hid a magic necklace that holds the power of immortality? Get your priorities sorted girl!"

Before Megan could reply, the archivist returned with another thick binder. "You were asking about St. Mary's Priory. We have this, which is a kind of housekeeping book for the Priory. It lists everything, from the crops the monks grew to rotas of who was saying mass. It's written in very old English, but you should be able to understand it."

Jamie hovered eagerly over it. "Fantastic! Now this might prove a thing or two. That monk's name was Friar Lucius wasn't it?

"Yes," Megan answered, adding under her breath, "As if you didn't know."

****

They worked all morning, pouring over the ancient books that were so difficult to decipher, and while Megan found it all very interesting, there was nothing to link her with the town's history. She'd been the daughter of a stonemason, hardly worthy of being mentioned in history books.

Jamie however, seemed entranced. "Hey, look at this. This priory record book is brilliant. Here's some stuff about the monks. It's dated July twelve hundred and twenty-two. That's not far off our estimated date is it?"

Freya peered over his shoulder. "How can you decipher that scrawl?"

"You get used to it. Look, there's a Friar Marcus mentioned. Hey, he must have been the chef. He's written loads about the food he's cooked, turnips, carrots, bread. And here's another — Friar Edward. Oh wow! This is fascinating stuff!"

"No Lucius then?" Megan couldn't resist asking.

"Not so far, but look, they spent two shillings and three pence on cloth for the making of new robes... and what's this... income... one shilling and nine pence from the sale of a barrel of mead. Bargain!"

"Do they have a loo in here?" Freya interrupted him.

"Yes, just out there on the right," Jamie said, hardly breaking off from reeling out listings from the book. "And here's a rota, looks like it's showing which monk was taking early and late prayers and stuff."

"Back in a tick," Freya announced, heading through the glass doors.

"This is ace," Jamie ranted on, totally absorbed. "And listen to this... twelfth of March in the year twelve hundred and twenty-one they welcomed a novice monk into the priory. His name was Henry... I've always had the feeling that my name was Henry in those days. I mentioned that to you didn't I, Celeste? Henry after the king."

Megan's skin crawled. He was still chattering on, totally unaware of what he'd just called her — Celeste!

"Your name, child? What is your name?

"Celeste."

He had carved it into his soul.

"Y... you know what Jamie," Megan said, trying desperately to sound normal. "I'm going to see if Freya wants to take a break and get something to eat. We'll see you later." She didn't wait for a reply, but hurried out of the room, bumping into Freya in the corridor and dragging her out into the sunshine. Jamie's voice was still ringing in her ears... *Celeste!*

****

Jamie was barely aware that they'd left him on his own. The thirteenth century was absorbing him, calling him, dragging him back into the past. He read on, page after page, deed after deed. Name after name.

Turning yet another parchment-like page, he stared down at the words written in old English.

Over and over he read them — until they were emblazoned into his brain.

"Look at this!" he finally exclaimed before remembering the girls had gone for food. He fished out his mobile anxious to tell them what he'd discovered. It was still on camera mode — and the image of Megan and Freya he'd taken earlier.

He went to switch to Contacts to ring Freya, but instead did a double take on the photo.

There were people in the background behind the girls. One person stood out amongst all the others. A tall, thin figure, dressed in a black hooded robe.

Jamie staggered as memories of a life lived eight hundred years ago came flooding back. His head swam. How could he have forgotten — how could he? And that face — that stark evil face...

The clattering of his phone dropping to the floor brought the archivist running.

Lucius was alive — and here!

****

The precinct was bustling with shoppers — people doing their normal everyday things. Shopping, browsing, chatting, but Megan's head was spinning.

"Megan! Will you slow down? What's wrong? What's happened?"

"He called me Celeste," she answered, glancing back over her shoulder, afraid that she'd find him coming after her.

"You must have told him at some time. It was probably just a slip of the tongue."

"I've never told him — at least not in this life. Did you?"

Freya shrugged. "I don't think so."

"Think hard Freya. Did you ever mention my medieval name to him?"

Freya thought for a moment then shook her head. "No. No I didn't."

Megan surged on, needing to get well away from Jamie. "That proves it then. Jamie and Lucius are the same person."

"No! I can't believe that," Freya said practically running to keep up with her. "Jamie and I have been friends for so long."

"He's been pretending to be your friend, waiting for me to show," Megan tried to explain.

"But I've known him since we were kids," Freya argued. "Besides, if Jamie is Lucius, who's that ghostly monk who's been haunting you and whispering in your ear? If Lucius has been reincarnated as Jamie, he can hardly be a ghost creeping through your wall at the same time, can he?"

"That must have been my imagination," Megan admitted, realising the streets were cobbled now, and she had to glance towards the shopping precinct to check she hadn't slipped back in time again. "Maybe those words, *where did you hide it*, were the last words I ever heard in that life. That's why they're haunting me."

Freya caught hold of her arm as the ruins of the old cathedral loomed up ahead. "What if it's all imagination?" she asked softly.

"If only it was," Megan murmured gazing up at the ruins. "But it's real, and the Cross of Aes Dana is hidden up there in the brickwork. Freya, don't you see the power the cross possesses? It's protected the spire all these years, not even bombs and fire could bring it down."

Freya glanced unhappily at her. "Its solid brick Megan, built to last. Everything that could burn in the Blitz, burned."

"You're wrong, it's the Cross of Aes Danas that's protected the spire," argued Megan.

Freya smiled kindly and gave her a hug. "Then we need to work out what we're going to do, because I don't think we can sort this out on our own. I think we might need some sort of religious help. Like an exorcist or something."

Megan shuddered. "That makes it sound even creepier than it is. Maybe we should have a word with the priests here at the cathedral first."

Freya thought for a moment then agreed. "It's worth a try. Shall we see if we can find anyone in the new cathedral?"

"What have we got to lose?" Megan said, trying to smile. Linking Freya's arm they hurried around the ruins.

Approaching the vast new cathedral, Megan stood for a moment in awe at the sight of the impressive building and gigantic statue of Saint Michael overpowering Satan. Still gazing at it, they went up the wide modern steps to the paved area that linked the old and the new cathedrals, and mingled with the tourists.

"I'm not quite sure what to say..." Megan began but stopped abruptly as a woman tourist close by suddenly screamed.

The girls spun round to see a black swirl of evil leaping from the top step, arms outstretched, black robes flapping like the wings of a bird of prey swooping down on its helpless victim.

People scattered.

Megan stood riveted to the spot as eight hundred years melted away as if in the blinking of an eye.

Chapter Nineteen
Quest For Immortality

Too shocked to scream, Megan looked up into the sharp evil eyes of Friar Lucius as they darted left and right before settling on her. She heard his deep sigh of satisfaction from where she stood.

Freya was dragging on her arm. Megan was barely aware of her. All she could think of was that Lucius was here — in all his demonic glory. Not in the guise of a schoolboy but as a medieval monk who had somehow followed her through time to get the one thing he craved — the power of immortality.

"Megan, run!" Freya begged, pulling frantically at her arm.

"There's nowhere to run," Megan breathed, standing her ground as Lucius strode towards her.

His black robes billowed out as he forged forward, arrogantly barging tourists aside without a second glance. One man challenged him only to be pushed roughly to the ground and when another tried to confront him, he too was thrown mercilessly aside.

"Is it Lucius?" Freya breathed.

Megan nodded, her heart pounding with utter terror as she stared at that gaunt white face beneath the cowl.

Lucius composed himself as he saw Megan standing there, facing him. Slowly, he brought his hands up and together, as if joined in prayer as he lowered his head. Then slowly and purposefully he walked towards Megan.

Megan felt her heart thudding against her ribcage as he closed the space between them. Nearby she was vaguely aware that Freya was pleading with people to help. Another man stepped forward and was instantly sent flying by the monk's flaying arm.

And then Lucius reached her and stood just a breath away from her. Megan heard the swish of ancient cloth, and smelled the cloying smell of death.

He breathed a long, heavy sigh of satisfaction, as if he had waited a long, long time for this moment. "Celeste! I have watched and waited for you, and now you have kindly returned." He stretched his neck towards her, so that his white bloodless face was an inch from hers, wreaking the stench of death and evil as he said, "I believe you have something to tell me. Where did you hide it?"

Megan met his stare. She glared up into those black soulless eyes and answered defiantly. "You will never, ever know. I went to my grave last time keeping the secret safe and I'm willing to do it again. I'll never tell you!"

"Such bravery from a small, insignificant child," he sneered, thrusting aside another man who was trying to intervene. "Even though you know the lengths I will go to, to acquire this power of immortality."

"Why do you need a magical pendant?" Megan demanded, terror forcing her to stand up to him. "You died eight hundred years ago yet you're still here."

His face contorted with fury. "Yes! Because of you, my body was cast to the worms centuries ago. But my sworn oath as I swung from those gallows never to rest until the cross was mine, allowed my soul to remain here, earthbound, until the cross was discovered by some unsuspecting mortal. Imagine my delight when you re-appeared after such a long wait."

Megan backed away, her voice trembling. "What are you? Ghost? Human?"

He looked pleased with himself. "For eight hundred years I have been hiding in the darkest of spirit worlds. But since your return I have mustered up all my energies and called upon every demon that stalks the shadows to grant me another spell of mortality." He extended his arms, gazing down at himself in sheer delight. "Without the cross I expect this new body of mine will last only one lifetime. With the cross, I shall live forever. And happily, I understand they do not hang murderers these days."

"They might make an exception for you!" she cried defiantly.

Her words were barely out before he grabbed her and thrust a dagger against her throat. A long, thin deadly sharp blade with an ornate bone handle. Megan gasped as a sensation of *déjà vu* washed over her. He had pulled this knife on her before. She remembered clearly how he had confronted her after she had hidden the cross, eight hundred years ago. It felt like yesterday.

People screamed. Others scrambled for their mobiles, frantically making emergency calls.

Lucius held her tight, his powerful arm around her throat as the sharp point of steel touched her skin. All around, a sea of horrified faces gaped at her.

His voice was menacing as he rasped into her ear. "Where did you hide it?"

Talitha's voice echoed through her mind. *Hide it away forever, so that no one can use it — especially those who seek power and would do evil — untold evil for ever more. Evil that no mortal soul will be able to stop.*

"I'm not telling you!" Megan gasped, struggling to

breath.

His grip tightened. "Then I shall kill you... for the sheer pleasure of it."

Freya suddenly leapt forward, desperation in her eyes. "No! Don't hurt her! I'll tell you!"

"Freya, no! Don't tell him!"

His grip loosened. "Well, well, look who is here. The baby sister, reunited after so long."

"Let her go," Freya demanded, standing bravely up to him. "Let her go and I'll tell you."

His arms sprang open and Megan staggered free. "Freya, no! Please don't tell him. I made a promise."

Like cat and mouse, Lucius grabbed Megan again. "One of you should tell me before I get angry."

Someone else screamed. A woman in the crowd started to cry and beg him not to hurt them. "Tell him what he wants to know, for mercy's sake. Tell him!" the woman shrieked.

"I'm so sorry, Megan!" Tears were already streaming down Freya's cheeks as she turned to Lucius and murmured, "It's hidden in the spire, in the brickwork."

"Finally!" Lucius uttered, his cold eyes rolling up inside his head. "Finally!"

"So let her go," Freya cried, tears streaming from her eyes. "I've told you, haven't I?"

"Yes indeed," he answered and Megan felt him breathe a sigh of satisfaction, a sigh that he had bottled up for eight hundred years.

But then she felt his chest expand and his hand suddenly gripped the scruff of her neck like pinchers. She yelped as he swung her roughly around and frog-marched her up the steps into the ruins of the old cathedral and towards the spire.

"Let her go!" Freya screamed, running alongside, pulling on his arm, clawing at his robe, pummeling him furiously in an effort to make him release her.

At any second Megan expected him to send her reeling

like he'd done with everyone else who had got in his way. What she didn't expect was for him to twist the dagger in his hand to capture Freya in his other arm, holding them both captive, the blade thrust against Freya's throat now.

"Always so loyal, your little sister," he rasped as he marched along, forcing them to run. "I envy that."

As they were pushed across the open expanse of the cathedral ruins towards the entrance to the spire, two policemen came running towards them. Lucius' step didn't even falter and the policemen skidded to a halt as they saw the dagger pressed against Freya's throat. Lucius jerked his head, indicating that they let them pass.

Reluctantly, they moved aside and Megan saw the desperate expressions on their faces as they realised they had a hostage situation on their hands.

The woman in the kiosk at the bottom of the spire made a feeble effort to stop them going past, but one menacing glance from the monk reduced her to a quivering wreck.

He released Freya to go up the narrow spiraling staircase first. She staggered and then began climbing, sobbing quietly as she went.

Megan swung round to face up to him. "Let my sister go. This is nothing to do with her."

"You think not?" he sneered, jabbing her in the back as an indication to start climbing.

Megan's head spun. Eight hundred years ago she had been in this exact same spot, clutching a sacking package containing her father's mallet and chisel — and the Cross of Aes Dana. Now all her worst fears had come true. Lucius was here; he knew where she had hidden the cross. She had failed Talitha and put her sister in mortal danger too.

"We are wasting time," he uttered, his breath hot and rancid on her neck. "Although once I have the cross I shall have all the time in the world."

Megan climbed the worn stone steps, the feel of the cold

damp sandstone against her hand making her feel it was just moments ago that she had trod these stairs, not hundreds of years ago. Glancing down at her feet she saw the little canvas button up shoes, felt the rustle of her dress swishing against her legs.

In an instant she was wearing trainers and jeans again, but the monstrosity that had followed her from those past dark days was right behind her, the murderous dagger clutched in his hand.

She climbed slowly, trying to think what to do. Her only hope was to try and get the Cross of Aes Dana before he could get his hands on it.

The gloom of the narrow stairway brightened as they reached the top. The breeze was chilly with being so high and as Megan walked out she felt her head spin. The horizon had changed so much since she last stood here, but still she could see the gentlest of curves, proving that the world wasn't flat.

But how very different the view was from the last time she stood here. Now there were no fields to be seen. A sprawling city spread as far as the eye could see. Tower blocks, shops, roads, houses, concrete, glass, chimneys, a few trees. The sound of sirens echoed up from the streets below.

Lucius walked to the balcony wall and looked down, his robes billowing in the breeze. And then he swung around, his eyes burning through Megan's. "At last, Celeste, I will ask you finally... where did you hide it? And I warn you, if I have to ask you one more time, I shall use this dagger on your little sister — and you know I mean it."

Megan saw the terror in Freya's eyes and her heart broke. "Don't touch her! I'll show you."

Lucius' dark eyes shifted from one girl to the other, as if detecting some trick. And then he shrugged and Freya inched her way back towards the staircase. He rubbed his hands together.

"Celeste, I warn you. Do not waste time by telling me

you cannot recall where you hid it, because I will not believe you."

With a defiant glare Megan walked to the north-facing wall, her eyes fluttering downwards to the brickwork. Her gaze rested on the brick. She knew it instantly even though it looked so like every other brick. Kneeling down, she saw the shafts of sandstone that she'd chipped at to ensure a close fit after lodging the cross behind it.

She could barely believe that it looked exactly as she had left it eight hundred years ago. It could have been yesterday. "I need something to dig it out with."

"Would you care to use my dagger?"

"Yes, that would work," she answered knowing he had no intention of handing over his weapon.

"You think I am that stupid?" he snarled, swooping down over her like a hawk devouring its prey. Twisting her arms behind her back to hold her with one hand, he used his dagger to gouge out the brickwork, scraping away the years of dust and moss that had gathered.

Held captive, unable to move, the grating sound of brick sent Megan's thoughts whirling back hundreds of years. It seemed no time since she had knelt here, chipping away at this brick, her heart pounding.

But now her heart pounded for another reason. What if she hadn't chosen well? What if the cross was long gone? If that was the case, she had no doubt how Lucius would vent his anger.

She held her breath as he moved the half brick aside and reached into the cavity. He turned his face to look at her, gloating, his black eyes sparkling with desire. From far away came the sounds of police and ambulance sirens.

Slowly he brought his hand out from the cavity and opened his bony fingers.

A small cross, covered in gemstones, the iron green with age, lay there in the palm of his hand. Megan's thoughts spiraled crazily at the sight of the Cross of Aes Dana. It had been so long since she'd seen it. So many years had gone by.

"Finally!" he breathed, his face lighting up as he slipped the chain over his head, easily avoiding Megan's desperate attempt to grab it. "Immortality is mine!"

He rose to his feet, turning aside from Megan as if she were no longer of any importance. "Now I am untouchable, invincible... immortal!"

"I'm so sorry," Freya sobbed.

Megan could see the transformation in him, the power of the pendant was seeping into him, he looked immortal — and utterly, utterly evil.

Freya reached for her hand, trying to pull her towards the stairs as he paraded around the balcony wallowing in his newfound powers. Megan remained rooted to the spot, staring at him in horror.

"Who can touch me now? No one!" he declared. "I can take whatever I desire. I can gather an army around me that will make other armies look like infants, and I will show no mercy. I will wipe out anyone who stands in my way. It has been worth the wait. At last, I, Lucius, possess this cross..."

"Let's hope it hasn't lost its magical powers then!"

Megan spun round at the sound of Jamie's voice.

Jamie emerged from the stairway and boldly walked straight towards Lucius, positioning himself between the monk and the girls like some gallant warrior. A warrior in a silly T-shirt with a penguin on the front.

"Jamie!" Megan gasped, her knees buckling but her heart soaring at the sight of him. She had linked the two together, Jamie and Lucius... but she was wrong, so very wrong!

Relief flooded through her and with it another sensation of *déjà vu*.

"You!" Lucius snarled, stopping in his tracks, his eyes spearing Jamie with hatred.

Megan reeled as a memory unfolded in her mind. This

wasn't the first time Jamie had intervened between her and Lucius. The sudden sensation of *déjà vu* that swept over her was overwhelming.

She could picture him, all those years ago. Time flew back. Images flashed vividly into her mind... running home after hiding the cross... Lucius barring her way... the dagger... And then, from the direction of the village came a young monk — and her little sister, Ruth hot on his heels.

No wonder Jamie had memories of being a monk. He wasn't Lucius reincarnated at all. It was Jamie and the young monk who were one and the same. The monk who had accompanied Lucius into their village on the morning Talitha died. The young monk she had bumped into in the church that evening when she had gone to hide the cross. Not Lucius...

As if time was standing still, Megan visualised the events as if they had happened yesterday — Lucius lunging at her with that blade — and the young monk defending her. Her head swam. No wonder Jamie had seen so much blood, no wonder!

It had been his blood that he'd seen. His life's blood — ebbing away.

"Jamie be careful!" Megan screamed, terrified that history was about to repeat itself. "He's got a knife!"

Lucius' face twisted with fury. "Henry Craven! Did you not learn your lesson the last time?"

"You look pathetic," Jamie mocked, standing indolently, arms folded. "That cross is nothing but an ancient old relic. Were you really taken in by those myths?"

Lucius' thin mouth curled into an ugly sneer as he slipped the dagger out from the folds of his robe. "I cut you down once before, Henry Craven, I will gladly do it again. I'm sure Celeste will enjoy seeing your blood spilt a second time."

Although sick with fear, Megan couldn't let Jamie do this alone. Trembling from head to toe, she stepped forward and stood shoulder to shoulder with him ignoring Freya's frantic pleading for them to run. "Jamie's right!" she stated boldly. "That old cross has no more super powers than my little finger. I was just doing what I was told. Talitha told me to hide it, so I hid it. I've no idea what powers it's supposed to possess. For all I know Talitha was just a story teller."

Lucius threw back his head and uttered a sound that no doubt was meant to be a laugh, but it sounded to Megan like it was coming from the depths of hell. "I almost admire your cunning, child. I suspect you'd like me to prove my immortality by handing you my dagger so you can thrust it through my heart, or maybe you would like me to leap over this balcony?"

"I doubt you have a heart — if you have it will be black," said Megan, tilting her chin defiantly.

"Yeah!" Jamie added, standing tall. "If you reckon you're immortal, prove it! Give me your dagger. You'll need to prove that pendant has super-powers or you'll never be sure."

Lucius' eyes flashed, and then, spinning the dagger in his hand, he pointed the handle towards Jamie and smiled coldly. "Take it then."

"It's a trick... be careful." breathed Megan, icy cold terror sweeping over her.

Hesitating just for a second, Jamie darted forward, snatching at the dagger, only to have Lucius spin it again, so that the blade was pointing at his heart. Freya screamed and Jamie dodged, ducking swiftly down at Lucius' knees and tackling him to the floor.

As the two struggled on the ground Megan leapt forward, desperately trying to stamp on Lucius' wrist to make him release the dagger. But in one powerful surge he thrust them both aside and they were slammed back against the sandstone wall. Megan felt the breath knocked out of her.

In a flash Lucius was back on his feet. "Pathetic worms!" he laughed, leaping up onto the turreted balcony wall, causing shrieks from bystanders hundreds of feet below as he teetered on the edge. He raised his arms to the heavens, his black robes billowing in the wind. "However, for you Celeste, so you will know that Henry Craven did not die in vain all those years ago..."

Jamie was back on his feet before her, edging nearer to the balcony. Megan followed, her heart pounding. Lucius was capable of anything, even throwing them all over the balcony if he wanted.

Somehow she remained defiant. She folded her arms, shifting her stance to look mockingly up at him, aware that by taunting him she could be signing her own death warrant. But in her heart she knew she couldn't run. She had to see this through to the end — one way or the other.

Jamie looked up at him balanced there on the narrow wall. Unimpressed, he shook his head slowly. "So your magic cross improves your sense of balance. Big deal!"

Lucius sneered down at them. "You want to know if I can cheat death? Shall I throw myself over? Shall I jump? Will I drop like a stone, or float like a feather?"

"Yeah, let's find out," Jamie goaded. "You don't look immortal to me! You look like a ghoul, not alive, not dead. You're a freak!"

The insult bounced off him and for a second he stood there, balanced perfectly. Then, bending his knees Lucius leapt.

For a moment he seemed to hover in mid-air, his face shining with evil. People below screamed. Megan held her breath.

He plummeted downwards and her heart soared. Surely no one, not even with a magical cross, could survive a three hundred foot drop onto concrete.

But then, to her horror, a second later, she spotted the claw-like fingers hooked over the balcony wall. She cried out in dismay as Lucius slowly pulled himself up so that his deathly white face appeared between the two turrets.

He smiled in evil delight as he hung there. "Fools! The cross doesn't give me the power of flight. Had I not caught hold of the wall I would have hit the ground like a stone but then, I would have simply got up and walked away, not a hair of my head harmed."

"Not without this pendant though!" Jamie cried, swiftly reaching over the balcony and grabbing the cross from around Lucius' neck.

Lucius' gloating sneer of triumph turned to fury — and then almost instantly, to stark and utter terror.

Jamie backed away and placed the Cross of Aes Dana around Megan's head, pushing her backwards, out of Lucius' reach as the monk scrambled in an attempt to drag himself over the wall.

It all happened so quickly that Megan stood open-mouthed. Clutching the cross, she stared at Lucius' stunned expression. Frantically, he tried to claw himself upward, but no mortal man could cling on by just his fingertips. Gravity was proving stronger than him. Slowly he began to slip.

His fingernails dug into the sandstone, making claw-marks, which lengthened as his own weight slowly dragged him downwards.

"Help me!" he gasped, his face contorted with terror. "Take my hand, Henry Craven. Help me! For pity's sake, help me!"

His bony hands were white, his veins standing rigid along his wrists. His eyes filled with desperation and fear, as if he could almost see hell's demons eagerly awaiting.

And then with one agonised shriek, he was gone, plummeting, screaming to the ground, with no chance this time to curse the world and vow to return.

Megan and Jamie peered over the wall. Lucius' black figure spiraled downwards, growing smaller and smaller, his scream becoming fainter. The crowd below scattered as he hurtled towards them. Then with a horrific *thud*, there was silence.

Lucius lay outstretched and motionless on the concrete far below.

Chapter Twenty
Hidden — Finally

Megan turned away from the sight of Lucius' shattered body.

Freya ran to her, wrapping her arms around her and hugging her fiercely. "Has he gone? Is he dead? Is it over?"

"Yes, it's over. Thank goodness," Megan said when she could breathe again. But her eyes were fixed on Jamie, still staring down over the turrets, scarcely able to believe that this boy had once died for her and would have given his life for her — again.

Freya peered over the wall then quickly recoiled, her face screwed into a grimace at the sight below. "Ugh! But I don't feel sorry for him. Megan, I was so scared…"

"We all were," Megan said softly, reaching over to touch Jamie's hand. "Thank you, Jamie. Thank you for standing up to him like you did — this time, and before. You gave your life for me…"

"What do you mean?" Freya asked, puzzled. "I don't understand."

As his fingers closed warmly around hers, Megan smiled

at Freya. "He saved me from Lucius in my old life. His memory of seeing blood — that was his blood. He tried to save me but he died in the process."

"At least now I understand," Jamie said, turning away from the sight on the ground. "That's what brought me here. I found something written in the archives. I went to ring you, Freya, but spotted the photo on my mobile that I took of you pair earlier."

"And?" Megan puzzled as he took his mobile phone out and showed them the image. Both girls gasped, seeing themselves and Lucius in the background.

Jamie continued. "As soon as I saw him it all came flooding back. I remembered being Henry, a novice monk when Lucius was a Friar. And you Freya. I remembered you — only you were called Ruth in those days. It even came clear what you were trying to tell me — that Lucius was looking for your sister. You were begging me to help her. Anyway, I've no idea how he became mortal again, but I guessed he was after you Megan so I thought I'd better find you — and quick."

"I'm just so glad you did, Jamie," Megan said, reaching up and wrapping her arms around his neck.

"So am I!" Freya exclaimed hugging him too. "Thank heavens you looked at that photo on your phone. What were you going to ring us about though?"

His arm remained around Megan's waist as he explained. "I'd found something in that ancient book, just a couple of lines. I can quote them though... I don't think I'll ever be able to forget them: Friar Lucius was hung by the neck until dead for the heinous act of stabbing unto death Henry Craven, a novice monk of the same Order."

Megan felt so ashamed suddenly. "And I thought you and Lucius were the same person."

Oddly, Jamie looked quite relieved. "Ah! So that's what had got into you. I thought I was just losing my charm."

"Never!" exclaimed Megan, hugging him and planting a

kiss on his cheek.

A smile spread across his face. "That's good to know."

Freya suddenly coughed. "Excuse me, but what are we going to do with the magic cross?"

"We have to hide it again," Megan said, easing free from Jamie's arms, realising they were wasting time. "The police will be up here any minute. They mustn't find it. No one must get their hands on this again. There'll be other people around like Lucius who would use it for evil. I have to hide it again, like Talitha asked me to do."

She worked swiftly, replacing the Cross of Aes Dana back into the cavity, slotting the shafts of brick back into place. Then, sweeping up the specks of red dust she released them over the turrets into the wind.

Only just in time. Moments later the sound of policemen's boots on the stone steps and laboured breathing echoed out from the spire archway.

"Our secret," Megan whispered to Jamie and Freya, holding both of their hands and walking towards the archway to meet the policemen. "The spire has kept the Cross of Aes Dana hidden for eight-hundred years. Let's hope it will do the same for the next eight hundred."

****

Coventry Telegraph Monday 22nd September:

Police today cordoned off the city centre when a Benedictine monk leapt to his death from the old cathedral spire after terrorising three local children. The youngsters escaped their terrifying ordeal unharmed. No apparent reason has been found for the monk's crazed actions.

Following day:

The Daily Mirror Tuesday 23rd September:

Forensic scientists have been brought in to investigate the

remains of a monk who died after jumping from a cathedral spire yesterday. Unconfirmed reports state that his body crumbled to dust within hours of his death. Investigations are ongoing.

About the Author

Ann Evans is an English writer with almost 20 books to her name. Most are books for young people but there have been a few romance novels too. Ann also writes non-fiction and was a feature writer for her local newspaper the Coventry Telegraph for 13 years. She also regularly writes magazine articles on all kinds of topics from animals to antiques. It was while researching an ancient church for an article that the idea for this book began to germinate in her head!

Ann began writing as a hobby when her three children were little. They are now all grown up with children of their own. Two of her five grandchildren are avid readers of her books – the other three are still too young.

18587057R00089

Printed in Great Britain
by Amazon